Haunting
House of
Horror

Kaye
Umansky

Illustrated by Chris Fisher

Hodder
Children's
Books

a division of Hodder Headline plc

Text Copyright © 1998 by Kaye Umansky
Illustrations copyright © 1998 by Chris Fisher

First published in Great Britain in 1998
by Hodder Children's Books

10 9 8 7 6 5 4 3 2 1

A Catalogue record for this book is available from the
British Library.

ISBN 0 340 67308 7

Printed and bound in Great Britain by
Clays Ltd, St Ives plc

Hodder Children's Books
A Division of Hodder Headline plc
338 Euston Road
London NW1 3BH

Contents

The Cast

Hamish - a hamster

Professor Wilheim Von Strudel - a guinea pig

Fritz - a hedgehog

Master Zeke Cropstealer - a vole

Septica - a squirrel

Gretchen - a mouse

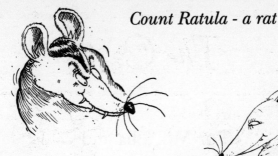

Count Ratula - a rat

Rodentia - another rat

Reg Parsley - a weasel

Thog - a mole

Ruben Parsley - another weasel

Luke Turnipburger - yet another weasel

For Mo, Ella and
all hamsters
everywhere

PROLOGUE

Picture it. A wild, wintry night. An icy wind moans around the walls of a mighty castle, which sits bang on top of a mountain. Snow, pine trees, a frost ringed moon - all the usual stuff.

In the Great Hall of the castle, candles flicker wildly in the draught. There are many things of interest, but for now we will focus on a large, ornately carved silver tureen sitting in the middle of a long, polished table.

A huge, spade-like, hairy paw descends from above and slowly lifts the lid. Steam pours forth in a great, white cloud, filling the air with the unmistakable odour of . . .

Tomato soup. Thick, red and gloppy.

There are two waiting to partake of this feast. They sit at either end of the table. They are served by a third - the owner of the hairy paw - who shuffles up and down between them, bearing steaming bowls.

Listen now to the conversation.

"How the wind moans. We are in for a storm."

"Yes."

(Silence, broken only by the tinkle of a spoon on the edge of a bowl.)

"Mmm. This is good. You are not hungry tonight, my dear?"

"No."

"You must eat. You must be at your best for our visitors. They will need entertaining."

"I know."

"Are you excited, my dear?"

"Of course."

"Good. I too am looking forward to having some fresh blood around the place. But, in the meantime, we must keep our strength up. So eat."

No more is said. The silence is broken only by the wind whistling around the castle walls, searching and crying to be let in.

CHAPTER ONE

SNOW
AND SANDWICHES

"Snow, snow, snow! How I loff ze snow. Snow to ze right of us, snow to ze left of us, everyvhere ees snow. Here snow, zere snow. Look up, vot do ve see? Snow. Look down - more snow. Is beautiful thing, zis snow, huh, Hamish?"

"What?" said Hamish, coming to with a start. He had been dreaming about being chased down a long corridor by a large prawn wearing a blue and white striped apron. For some reason, it was asking to borrow a pair of gardening gloves.

He yawned, rubbed his eyes and stared around blearily as he tried to remember where he was.

"Sorry? What did you say, Professor? Must have dozed off there for a moment."

Professor Von Strudel peered sadly over his glasses at the small, bundled up hamster sitting opposite. The lad was willing, but he had no staying power. Unlike guinea pigs, who were renowned for it. Relentless, were guinea pigs. He should know. He was one.

He gave a little sigh and began his speech again.

"Snow, snow, snow! How I loff ze snow. Snow to ze right of us, snow to ze left of us, everyvhere ees snow. Here, snow, zere, snow. Look up, vot do ve see?"

Hamish looked up at the luggage rack above his head.

"My lunch box? he said.

"I vos referring to snow," said the Professor, severely.

Hamish hastened to put right his mistake. He stretched out a paw and rubbed at the condensation on the carriage window pane.

"Snow, yes. Gosh, you're right, Professor. It certainly is looking rather snowy out there."

It was, too. Dark and snowy. The trouble was, it had been like that for hours and hours. It had been all right at first, but there was something very samey about snow seen through the window of a speeding train. After a while it tended to make you drop off and dream about prawns.

The Professor didn't think so, of course. Every interestingly shaped hummock, every frozen lake, every white capped mountain, every clump of pine trees sent him into transports of delight. The occasional fleeting glimpse of a tumbledown cottage, complete with glowering cottager out shovelling the front doorstep, brought on near hysteria. He was nothing if not enthusiastic.

But that was because he was brainy. Brainy types, Hamish had observed, seemed interested in *everything*.

Hamish gave himself a private little hug. He must be the luckiest hamster in the world. Out of all the applicants, Professor Von Strudel, world famous historian, had chosen him - yes, him! Hamish Barleycorn! - to be his assistant. Hamish Barleycorn, of whom Mrs Golightly, his teacher, had written: "Hamish tries hard. I, on occasions, have found him very trying indeed."

Hah, thought Hamish. If she could only see me now, speeding through the night, on my way to goodness knows what adventures.

Of course, it had helped that the Professor happened to be his godfather, and that Hamish's mum had written a letter begging him to give the lad a chance. And, as he found out later, there had only been two other applicants for the job: A cross-eyed gerbil with bad breath, and a stoat named Nobby who had just come out of prison and had ended his interview by running off with the Professor's ink well. Still.

"Are zere any of our delicious sandviches left, by any chance?" enquired the Professor hopefully.

"I think so," said Hamish. Actually, the sandwiches were his. His mum had packed them. The Professor, of course, hadn't thought to bring any food for the journey - but, hey, ho, that was typical of him. Head in the clouds, always thinking brainy thoughts.

Eager to be of use, Hamish climbed to his feet, steadied himself on the rocking train, stood on tiptoe and brought down his lunch-box. It was pink and had a picture of a hamster in a jolly sailor suit on it. He hated it.

"There's one," said Hamish, peering inside. "Dandelion, I think."

"Excellent!" beamed the Professor. "Dandelion, dandelion, how I loff ze dandelion."

Hamish handed it over and the Professor downed it in one. Being brainy and thinking lofty thoughts never seemed to affect his appetite, Hamish noticed.

"Ah! Zat hit ze spot. Sorry. Did you vant half, lad?"

"It's all right. I don't mind," said Hamish. He didn't, much. He had tried nibbling on a cheese roll earlier in the journey, but excitement had made his stomach queasy and he had tucked most of it into his cheek pouch for later. It was still there,   waiting to be savoured when the time was right.

He sat back down in his seat

"Tell me again," he said, "about the castle we're going to see."

"Ah! Castles, castles, how I loff castles!" murmured the Professor dreamily. He put his feet up on the vast, brass bound trunk that lay between them on the carriage floor. The trunk that was crammed full of books and mysterious pieces of equipment. The trunk Hamish had taken all night to pack and all day to get down the stairs.

"Take it from me, Hamish. You can never see too many castles in a lifetime. So much

15

history! So much romance! Every stone tells a story! I haff seen castles all over ze vorld. Spanish castles, French castles, leetle vuns, beeg vuns, all of zem I am putting in my book. Zis book vill be my masterpiece! Ze best sing since . . ." He waved his paws around, searching for the right phrase.

"Sliced carrot?" ventured Hamish. As far as he was concerned, nothing could beat it.

"Exactly! It vill be a collector's item, Hamish. All ze libraries vill haff copies. *Castles* by Professor von Strudel. Snappy title, eh?"

Hamish nodded, terribly impressed. His own writing experience was limited to compositions in school, with scorching titles like *What I did in my holidays* and *A Country Walk*. Since leaving school, he hadn't put pen to paper, apart from the occasional note for the milkmouse - and even then, his mum had been forced to point out that you don't spell pint with a Y.

"But zis castle zat we go to now," continued the Professor, scrabbling wildly beneath his cloak. "Zis castle, Hamish, vill be ze jewel in ze crown! So much mystery! So many secrets. Ze owner is a bit of a hermit, you know? Private type. Doesn't encourage visitors. Ve are most lucky to get ze invitation. Now, vere is zis invitation, I ask myself? Ah!"

Triumphantly, he produced a single sheet of paper from an inside pocket and waved it under Hamish's nose.

The paper bore a coat of arms at the top. On it, in curly black writing, was written:

Dear Professor Von Strudel,

After some thought, I agree to your request to include the Castle Ratula in your latest book. I understand that you will need to spend a few days here, studying the archeticture and making notes and so on and so forth. I shall expect you on Sunday, October 28th together with your new young assistant. I am sure you are right when you say that he will speed up your work. When one has been working on a project for some time, there is nothing like fresh blood to move things along.

Until then, I remain, sir, your faithful servant,

Count Ratula

"I had to write many times," said the Professor. "He ignore all my letters. It vos only ven he hear I have new, young assistant zat he finally say ve can come. You bring me luck, eh?"

"I hope so," said Hamish. "I'll do my best to help, Professor."

"Goot, goot." The Professor leaned across and patted him kindly. He was a good lad, this new assistant. A bit of a plodder, but you couldn't have everything. "Of course you vill. I teach you many things. Vatch, look and listen, and you go far. Ah ha! I think we slow down. Journey's end. See to ze trunk, zere's a goot lad."

He was right. The train was now crawling along. Through the window, despite the whirling snow flakes, Hamish could just make out the letters on a sign nailed to a wooden fence.

GROTZENBURGEN

That was the name of their destination. At long last, they had arrived!

Icy snowflakes bombarded them as they climbed stiffly from the train onto the small platform. The Professor went first, carrying his walking stick. Hamish came after, wrestling with his own backpack, the lunch box, an umbrella (which his mum had insisted upon) and, of course, the Professor's massive trunk.

There were no other visitors for the little mountain village of Grotzenburgen. As might have been expected in a remote hamlet of its size, there was no porter either.

The Professor wasn't in the least bit put out by the dark, icy loneliness of it all.

"Aaaaah!" he said, raising his nose and twinkling his whiskers with appreciation. "Smell zat fresh mountain air, Hamish. Fresh air, fresh air, how I loff ze fresh air!"

And he strode off towards the ticket office with Hamish toiling along behind, all hung up with bags and stuff and dragging the huge trunk in his wake.

There was nobody about. Just a small, hastily scrawled note on the window. It said, GONE FOR LUNCH. TUESDAY 11.45 a.m.

"Must have been a good one," remarked

Hamish. "It's taken him six days already. Lots of courses."

They stepped out through the small station exit. Behind them, the train let out a warning whistle and a blast of steam, then slowly moved away.

That's that, then, thought Hamish, with a little thrill of anticipation. No going back now.

A bitterly cold wind blustered down the narrow street. Hamish reflected that Grotzenburgen was a very big name for such a tiny place Two rows of small wooden houses stood on either side, their roofs groaning under the weight of the snow. All had darkened windows. There was no sign of life anywhere. But then, of course, it *was* late. Everyone was probably fast asleep in bed.

"Now what?" asked Hamish, doubtfully. He had been rather hoping that somebody would be there to meet them. It was unlikely that the Professor had given the matter any thought. Practical things just weren't in his line.

"Ve valk," said the Professor firmly. "It do us good. Ve valk through village until ve find ze local hot spot. Zen ve make enquiries."

He settled his hat more firmly on his head and set off, muttering, "Valk, valk, how I loff to valk!" and showing every evidence of great enjoyment.

Hot spot? thought Hamish doubtfully, brushing the snow from his whiskers. He expects to find a *hot spot* here?

With a little shiver, he settled his scarf more snugly around his neck and followed the Professor, the trunk slithering along behind him on the impacted snow.

The village was as silent as the grave. Shutters were firmly closed. No smoke issued from any of the chimneys. The only sound to be heard was the low moaning of the wind, the crunch of their footsteps and the grinding, rasping sound the trunk made as it slithered and slipped along behind.

"Sssssh!" said the Professor, coming to a sudden halt. "Listen!"

Hamish listened. At first, nothing. Then, mixed in with the wind, he heard it. The high, plaintive wail of a mouth organ!

CHAPTER TWO

DRINKS AND DOOM

A FIRE BURNED IN THE HEARTH OF THE THREE Ferrets Inn. The chimney evidently needed sweeping, for the atmosphere was heavy with smoke. Oil lamps were set high in niches in the stone walls, casting murky pools of light on the dismal scene.

A handful of customers sat drinking at the rough wooden tables. Nobody spoke. A trio of morose looking weasels slouched on a bench before the hearth, staring down at the rush strewn floor. The smallest one was noisily chomping his way through a bagful of termite-flavoured crisps. He wasn't sharing, although from his glum expression he didn't appear to be enjoying them much.

A wrinkled old squirrel, dressed in black from head to toe, sat huddled in a corner, mumbling to herself and taking the occasional slurp from a pint mug containing something black and frothy. Her tattered tail was curled around her shoulders for warmth. On her lap was a large, battered handbag.

Leaning against the bar was a solitary hedgehog, wearing leather breeches and a shabby old hat. He was blowing mournful chords on a harmonica, pausing only to sigh heavily and take an occasional slurp of ale.

Behind the bar stood a stout vole in a red velvet waistcoat. Every so often, he would give a vague swipe at the stained surface with a grubby cloth.

A small, grey mouse wearing an embroidered skirt and matching headscarf was moving briskly between the tables, collecting up glasses and empty nutshells.

Suddenly, the door flew open with a crash and a mini blizzard swept in on the back of a howling wind. The oil lamps flickered and the rushes swirled about the floor. The hedgehog's mouth fell open and his harmonica dropped with a little splash into his beer.

"Ah ha!" said a loud, cheery voice. "Inns, inns, how I loff zese rustic inns! Ze legendary hospitality of honest country folk! Ze heaped platters of simple but so delicious country fare!"

You could have heard a nut drop. All eyes bored into the stranger.

The Professor wiped the snow from his spectacles and beamed around the room.

"So!" he said. "Vere are ze ferrets?"

The weasel with the crisps bit down on the one that was already in his mouth. It sounded like a gun shot in the heavy silence.

"No ferrets 'ere," said the vole at length, when things were beginning to get embarrasing.

"No? But ze sign distinctly say Ze Sree Ferrets!" insisted the Professor, who was not easily put off.

"That's as maybe," growled the vole. "But that's just what tiz called. There idden no ferrets. I should know. I be the landlord of this establishment. Zeke Cropstealer. That be me."

"In zat case, you should change ze name, don't you sink?" said the Professor breezily. "Call it Ze Vun Vole. Zen zere is no confusion. But no matter, no matter. Ferrets, voles, vot do I care as long as I can get a drink, ha ha! A pint of your best barley beer, Master Cropstealer, and a glass of tomato juice for my young friend here. Is zat all right, Hamish? Tomato juice?"

"Er - fine," murmured Hamish, sidling in, uncomfortably aware of the stares. He wondered whether he should bring in the luggage but decided to let it take its chances in the snow. He had a feeling the Professor's trunk wouldn't be welcome. The place seemed quite full enough with just the Professor. Besides, with any luck, it might get stolen.

He quietly shut the door and stood with his back to it, fiddling with his scarf.

"Now!" cried the Professor. "A glance at your menu, my friend. For myself, I fancy a bowl of hot mash. Nussing special, just a little cereal and small pieces of wholewheat bread mixed viz a little hot vater. Zat should keep ze cold out, eh?"

"Us don't do food," said the vole firmly. He stood with his paws spread out on the bar, making no attempt at getting the drinks.

"No *food?* But vot are all zese bunches of garlic doing here?"

A coal fell from the fire. Somewhere, a clock ticked. The vole's eyes flicked furtively to and fro and he licked his lips.

"What garlic?" he said after a bit.

The Professor pointed to the rafters. Huge bunches of garlic dangled from hooks.

Long loops of it were hung like Christmas paper chains across the windows and over the lintel of the door.

"*Zat* garlic," he said. There was another pause. All eyes were on the vole.

"Decoration," he said, shortly.

"Oh, I *see*. Most unusual. I myself vould go for ze jolly balloons, but each to his own, eh? Now. To business. Haff you nussing cold? Some sliced sausage, perhaps?

"Nope."

"A small bowl of freshly cut grass clippings?"

"Nope."

"Tossed clover leaf salad viz French dressing?"

"Nope."

It was a real battle of wills. The Professor fired one last shot.

"A bag of crisps, zen? I see ze chappy over zere has some." He pointed triumphantly at the smallest weasel, who snarled and clutched the half empty packet to his chest in a defensive kind of way.

"Last packet. Reg got it," said the vole shortly.

The Professor finally admitted defeat. "Deary me, it seems ve are unlucky, Hamish. Never mind, never mind. Ve just stick viz ze drinks, zen."

For a long moment, Hamish thought the vole was going to refuse. But then, with an air of reluctance, he turned his back and began to busy himself with glasses and bottles.

The atmosphere relaxed a fraction. The weasels began to talk amongst themselves in a low undertone and the old squirrel took a slurp from her brimming mug. The small mouse took her trayful of glasses behind the bar and began to rinse them under a running tap. With a deep sigh, the hedgehog fished his harmonica out of his glass, wiped it on his sleeve and played an experimental minor chord.

"Music!" cried the Professor, instantly brightening up." Music, music, how I loff ze music! Zat' s right, come on, give us a tune! A merry folk dance, jah? All zat jolly hopping stuff, viz ze bells and ze funny trousers!"

"Fritz don't play that kind o' music," the vole informed him severely. "Us don't go in for jolly hoppin' round these parts."

"No? Zen vot kind of music do you play, Fritz?"

The hedgehog gave him a long, sad look.

"You want to know what Oi plays?" he said, in a slow, deep voice, that made you think of graveyards, worms under rotting logs and empty woods on foggy mornings. "Oi plays the koind o' moosic that'll send shivers down yer back bone an' make yer weep an' wail like a new born babby. That's the koind o' moosic Oi plays."

"*Really*?" said the Professor, fascinated. "And vot key vould zat be in? Do you haff a copy of ze lyrics, by any chance? I am a bit of a singer meinself. Ve can do a duet. Vot you say?"

The small mouse gave a little snigger.

The Professor gave her a solemn wink.

"Get on with your work, Gretchen," instructed the vole sharply.

The hedgehog continued to stare darkly for a moment longer, then put the harmonica back in his pocket, turned his back and took a long pull at his beer.

"Oh vell," said the Professor, with a little shrug. " Perhaps later."

"That'll be two schilling," the landlord informed him, dumping two glasses on the counter.

Hamish had charge of the money. The Professor, he had learned from bitter experience, was hopeless when it came to financial matters. He never counted his change, got coins mixed up and was always mislaying his purse. After several embarrassing episodes involving surly taxi drivers and impatient newpaper vendors, they had mutually agreed that it would be best if Hamish took care of the funds.

He scrabbled in the purse, counted out the required coins and placed them on the bar.

The vole swept them up in silence and threw them in the till. The Professor took a hearty swig of his drink, smacked his lips and beamed around.

"So qvaint!" he remarked in a loud stage whisper that bounced off the walls. "Zese rural types, viz ze amusing shorts. Ze creaky old beams. Ze smoke. Ze sooty valls. Ze intriguing vay ze feet stick to ze floor. Charming, eh, Hamish?"

"Mmmm," said Hamish, sipping his tomato juice. His eyes were on the ancient squirrel in the corner. She had taken a small, battered box from her handbag. Slowly, she lifted the lid and began laying out some tiny, yellowish objects in a circle on the table. She kept shooting him meaningful little glances, then looking back down at her arrangement, shaking her head and making tutting noises.

He gave the Professor a nudge.

"Look," he muttered under his breath. "What's she doing, do you think?"

The Professor followed his gaze.

"Aha!" he said, knowingly. "Superstition, Hamish. You get a lot of zat in zese remote places. Zey are breeding grounds for ze mysterious myths and ancient legends and strange beliefs. If I am not mistaken, vot ve haff here is ze local toothsayer."

"Don't you mean soothsayer?"

"No. I say vot I mean. Look. Vot has she got before her?"

Hamish looked. Then it hit him. Of course. Teeth! That's what those little yellow objects were!

"Golly," he said.

"Passin' through?" enquired the vole. For him, this verged on pleasant small talk, and the Professor was quick to take advantage.

"Vell, yes, my goot vole, you could say zat. Ve are, how you say, ze sheeps zat baas in ze night. In fact, ve are after directions. Perhaps you could help us? Ve are seeking a castle. Ze Castle Ratula, zat is ze name. Ve are ze guests of His Excellency ze Count. Perhaps you know him?"

The response was electrifying. The mouse froze with a tea-towel in a glass. The three weasels gave a united gasp. The hedge-hog's drink slipped through his paw and shattered on the floor. Meanwhile, the vole was backing away, holding up two crossed paws, his eyes wide with horror. But the most dramatic reaction of all came from the old squirrel in the corner.

"No, zir, no, zir, nivver say that name, zir! A curse be on them what sez that name!"

And with a wail, she hauled herself upright and came tottering forward, paws outstretched, and sank creakily to her knees before the surprised Professor. She grasped his paw in her own, and stared up at him, eyes rolling wildly in her sockets.

"Donee do it, zir! Donee take this poor young lad up there, zir. Not with it comin' up to the Eve of All Hallows an' all. 'Tiz madness, I tell 'e! Madness!"

"Get up, Septica, you've said enough," muttered the vole.

The squirrel ignored him. She was tugging away at the Professor's arm, trying to bring him down to her level. Obligingly, he leaned forward.

"The teeth, zir! I seen what's in the teeth!" she hissed into his ear. "They don't lie, zir. Doom! Doom an' misery! That's what they shows. Go yerself if yer must, but donee take the youngster up to that cold, cold place. 'Im with 'is bright eyes an' all that fresh young blood runnin' through 'is veins!"

"Zere, zere," said the Professor kindly, patting her vaguely with his free paw. "Don' t you vorry about Hamish. He von't catch cold. His mummy knit him nice voolly scarf, see?"

The small grey mouse gave a little snort. Hamish blushed. Then, much to his horror, the squirrel released the Professor and turned her attention to him!

"Beware!" she shrieked, scrabbling at his sleeve. Hamish attempted to back away, but the wall was in the way. "Beware of the Rat! Turn back, I tell 'e, before 'tiz too late . . ."

At a signal from the landlord, two of the weasels approached the frantic squirrel.

"You leave me be, Luke Turnipburger an' Reuben Parsley, I'll tell your mothers o' you, so I will . . ."

The weasels ignored her. They prised her paws loose, hauled her to her feet and firmly marched her back to her corner, where she slumped back in her chair and lapsed into low level snivelling.

Hamish looked dolefully down at his coat. It was a new one, bought specially in the sale. The squirrel's sharp claws had caused a couple of threads to come loose. His mum wouldn't be too happy about that. He looked up and caught the eye of the mouse. She rolled her eyes sympathetically at him and then continued to place the clean glasses on a shelf behind the counter.

"Take no notice of Septica," mumbled Zeke Cropstealer. "Her gets these funny turns from time to time."

He tapped his head in a meaningful way.

"Not at all, not at all!" cried the Professor. "Nussing like a funny turn, I alvays say. Laughter makes ze vorld go round, eh?

As a matter of fact, I used to do a funny turn myself, just for ze family, you know, at Christmas parties and so on. It vos a comical dance, had zem in stitches. Vot I do, I haff rose in my teeth and I put on lady's skirt and I take zese two saucepans, you know, and I put zem on my . . ."

"Professor," interrupted Hamish. "Do you think, perhaps, we should be going? It's just that it's getting awfully late, and with the snow and everything . . . ?"

"You're right, Hamish, of course you're right. Alvays ze practical vun, eh? Ve must avay! Sadly, our musical evening must vait until anuzzer time."

"You're quite set on it, then? Us could make you up a bed 'ere fer the night."

"Most kind of you, Master Cropstealer, but ve vouldn't dream of putting you to all zat trouble. Besides, our host is expecting us. If you could just point us in ze right direction?"

"Turn right up the street into the forest follow the track up the mountain can't miss it," muttered the vole shortly.

He came out from behind the bar armed with a broom and dustpan and began to sweep up the broken glass.

"I sank you," said the Professor. He downed the last of his beer. "Vell, all goot sings come to an end. Goot evening to you all, and sank you for your so delightful company. I feel I haff made good friends here. Ve shall return! And ven ve do, ve shall haff a jolly singsong, jah?"

And he took off his hat, bowed, replaced it and made for the door, with Hamish hurrying behind.

"Doom!" muttered the old squirrel behind his back. "Doom, I tell yer!"

Outside, the wind had eased off and the snow had ceased to fall. A pale moon swam from behind the clouds, turning the deserted street silver. It was still bitterly cold.

"Well!" said Hamish, stamping his toes. "That was a rum do. Funny lot, didn't you think?"

"Colourful," said the Professor. "Colourful rustic types, steeped in tradition. Ve may find ze vays of zese simple mountain folk a little strange, but no doubt zey sink ze same about us, arriving in ze dead of night in our smart city clothes, eh? Come. Let us go."

Hamish stared at the Professor's well worn cloak and shabby hat. Warm, yes. Comfortable, undoubtedly. But *smart*?

But then, of course, the Professor lived on a different planet to most animals. Brainy, you see.

Hamish wrapped his scarf around his nose, pulled his mittens on, struggled into his backpack, tucked the sandwich box under one arm, gripped the umbrella between his teeth, grasped hold of the handle of the trunk, which sadly had not been stolen after all and, with a little sigh, set off in the wake of the Professor, who was already a good way up the street.

He had hardly gone a few paces when the inn door opened again. Gretchen, the small mouse, stood there in a dim pool of light which spilled from within.

"Hey!" she said. "Catch!"

A small, round object came hurtling towards him. He let go of the handle and caught it in his gloved paws. *It was a head of garlic!* He looked up, astonishment in his eyes.

39

Just then, a heavy paw dropped onto the mouse's shoulder, whisking her back inside, and the door closed with a final sounding bang.

"Vot you got zere?" enquired the Professor, pausing in his stride.

"Garlic," said Hamish, bewildered.

"Garlic, garlic, how I - actually, I am not fond of garlic. But still. Is very kind thought. Very goot for colds, garlic. She care about you, Hamish. Perhaps she fancy you, eh?"

The Professor gave a hearty chortle and nudged him in the ribs.

"Don't be silly," said Hamish, going pink. And he thrust the garlic into his pocket, took hold of the handle and once again began to haul the trunk along the slippery street.

Behind them, the mournful strains of the harmonica started up again. Hamish couldn't be absolutely sure, but it seemed that the hedgehog was having a good old stab at *The Funeral March*.

CHAPTER THREE

CRISP WHISKERS AND A COLD CASTLE

HAMISH WAS BEGINNING TO SERIOUSLY HATE THE TRUNK. That's how he thought of it now. In capital letters. THE TRUNK. It was huge, heavy and had a mind of its own.

It hadn't been so bad going up the village street, but now they were in the forest it fought him every inch of the way. Despite his best efforts to keep it straight, it kept slithering sideways, hooking itself up on branches and tippling over into ditches.

In order to get a better purchase on it, Hamish tried hooking the curved end of his umbrella over the handle and tugging it like that. The advantage in this was not having to stoop so much. The disadantage was that he was now walking backwards. Also, his mittens

41

were slippery with frost and the pointy end kept slipping out of his paws.

"It's no good," he announced, after a few minutes of this. "There's got to be a better way."

"Hmm," said the Professor, vaguely. He stood ankle deep in snow, peering into the dark trees on either side and scribbling energetically into a small exercise book. He wasn't the least bit interested in luggage transportation. Practical problems like that were Hamish's department.

"Your walking stick's longer than my umbrella. I suppose I could jam the end of it under the lid and hook the curved end into my belt."

"Brilliant! You do, zat, Hamish. I leave it to you."

"Then at least I'd be facing the right way. But I don't suppose the lid'll close."

"Hmm. Hah! Do my eyes deceive me, or it zat ze rare *Abicus Voluminous* tree I am seeink over zere?"

"I suppose I could give it a try," pondered Hamish.

"No. My eyes deceive me. It is a pine tree.

Pity." The Professor took off his snowed-over spectacles, gave them a rub and replaced them. "I must be getting tired."

Hamish unclipped the lid, placed the rubber tip of the Professor's cane on the edge and slammed the lid down. Now the fastenings wouldn't close.

"Bother. What we need is a big weight on top. To keep it in place."

"Aha! Zere I can help you!" cried the Professor.

And he climbed on top, settled himself comfortably, erected Hamish's umbrella and beamed triumphantly.

"Zere. Now ve put ze uzzer sings on my lap, see? Leaving you free to do ze pulling, vhile I observe ze local flora. Togezzer ve haff solved ze problem. Mush!"

With a little sigh, Hamish hooked the curved end of the walking stick into his coat belt, faced forward and moved off.

Actually, it worked quite well. THE TRUNK was heavier now, of course, but at least he was facing the right way and his paws were free.

The further into the forest he went, the

deeper the snow. Despite his stout walking boots, the going was tough. Pine trees clustered darkly on either side of the steep, narrow trail. Every so often, little avalanches of snow would slither from the overburdened branches with a soft, plopping noise. It was bitterly cold. Lonely, too.

To take his mind off things, he began to talk. Little, gasping sentences, about the train journey and the peculiar goings-on at the inn. About his teacher, Mrs Golightly. About the time Stumpy McFeral and his gang of stoats had pinched his lunch box and thrown it in a puddle. About his favourite pudding (tinned pears). About the dream with the prawn. Anything that came into his mind, really. At first, the Professor made all the right interested noises, but after a while, he lapsed into silence. Hamish suspected he was asleep, but it was hard to tell in the dark.

He carried on talking anyway. The sound of his own voice was better than no sound at all.

"You see, the trouble with mum is . . . (gasp) . . . she treats me like I' m still a baby," he was saying as he toiled up the slope. "I told her . . . (gasp). . . I said, look, mum, I said, I'm a working animal now. I've got an important job.(Gasp, gasp, gasp). I'm going to be the Professor's right hand hamster, I said . . . (heave, gasp, strain). I've got to look the part. I don't *want* my mittens dangling down my coat sleeves on a bit of string. You can understand that, can't you, Professor?"

Silence.

"And then there was the business with the lunch box. I've had it since I was *three*, for goodness' sake. I begged her to buy me a new one . . . (Pant, pant, stop for a breather).

Please, mum, I said, buy a new lunchbox. I'll pay you back out of my first pay cheque. But would she? No. Don't you think that's unreasonable? Because I do."

Silence.

"And another thing," puffed Hamish, staggering on as the trail veered steeply to the left. "Another thing. She said I had to send her a postcard every day. Where am I supposed to get postcards from, out here in the middle of nowh–"

He broke off.

"Wow!" he said.

The trees had suddenly thinned out. Two massive, black wrought iron gates reared before him, entwined with snow-covered ivy and sealed shut with a rusty padlock. On either side, mounted on grey stone columns, were two great, crouching rats, carved in stone. Each one's jaws gaped open in a snarl, exposing rows of weather- worn, crumbling stone teeth. Their carved tails were coiled neatly around their feet. They looked ready to spring.

Below the statue on the right hand side, was a large stone set into the wall with a

carved inscription. Hamish could just make
out the letters:

Beyond the gates lay a driveway - a broad
sweep of fresh, untrampled snow. And there,
filling up the background, stood the castle.
High towers stretched like a witch's fingers
into the night sky, where a pale moon swam
in a sea of boiling clouds, bathing the scene
with a ghostly glow. Snow lay thickly on the
ramparts. Black windows stared accusingly
down at him, like hooded eyes.

"Wow!" said Hamish again. "What about that, then, Professor?"

Silence.

"Professor?"

He unhooked the walking stick, and waded back through the thick snow.

The Professor was sitting bolt upright. He still clutched the erect umbrella, but it had slipped back a little and was now leaning against his shoulder, providing no shelter from the elements. Snow had settled thickly on his hat. His face bore a glassy expression and his eyes stared straight ahead. A large icicle hung from the end of his nose.

Gingerly, Hamish reached out and tapped him on the shoulder.

There was a hard, tinkling sound. The sort of sound you would get if you tapped a glassful of iced lemonade.

"Oh dear," said Hamish, clapping a paw to his mouth. "Oh deary deary deary me!"

With a sense of deep forboding, he stood on tiptoe and touched the end of a whisker.

It was crisp!

The Professor was frozen solid!

Hamish stood rooted to the spot, thoughts racing wildly. There he was, stranded in the wild woods with locked iron gates barring his way and a deep frozen guinea pig on his paws. On top of everything else, it was beginning to snow again.

What in the world was he to do?

Just then, there was a faint hissing noise. He turned. To his astonishment, the gates now stood open! They had moved in complete silence, the bottoms just lightly brushing against the snow. The locked padlock - the one he had seen with his very own eyes - now hung open on the right hand gate!

How?

He didn' t stop to wonder. The situation was too serious He had to act, and quickly!

"Hold on, Professor," he shouted at the rigid shape. "I'll get help! I'll be right back! Think warm thoughts! Hot mash! Jolly hopping music! Deserts or something!"

And he ran through the gates and floundered up the driveway.

Several minutes later, breathing hard and with trembling knees, he was standing at the top of a flight of crumbling steps, pounding on an oak door with his small paws. It was like playing the drums with feathers.

Frantically he cast about for something hard to hammer with. A stone, a stick - anything.

It was then that his eyes fell upon the bell rope hanging to one side. In his panic, he had failed to notice it. He seized it with trembling paws and gave it an almighty tug.

From somewhere within, there came a distant clanging.

"Hurry!" he muttered, through chattering lips. "Hurry! Please, please, hurry!"

After what seemed like an eternity there came the sound of shuffling footsteps. With an agonizing slowness, they approached the door from the inside. Then stopped.

"Let me in!" squeaked Hamish, beside himself with frustration. "It's an emergency! Open up, *please!*"

There was a pause. In the next instant came the welcoming sound of heavy iron bolts being withdrawn, and the huge door swung slowly inwards.

A massive mole stood there, holding an oil lamp. Hamish had never seen a mole so big. His head almost touched the lintel. His arms bulged with muscles and seemed unusually long. They were displayed to advantage in a sleeveless leather jerkin. Around his waist was a thick, studded leather belt with a huge bunch of keys hanging from it. His breeches were patched and ragged.

There was something odd about his outfit, though. Something that didn't quite go. Hamish's eyes travelled down to the mole's feet.

They were stuffed into pink, fluffy slippers! This apparition stared down at Hamish through small, red rimmed eyes.

"Yersh?" he said. Actually, it sounded more like *yeeeerrrsh?* Slow and long drawn out; delivered in a gravelly voice.

"I need help!" squawked Hamish.

The urgency of the situation, together with the un-nerving appearance of this hulking great brute made his voice rise an octave. "My name is Hamish Barleycorn, and I'm Professor Von Strudel's assistant. The Count is expecting us. It's taken us rather longer than we expected to get here and I'm afraid there's been a bit of a disaster. The Profesor has been overcome with the cold. He's out there by the gate, frozen solid!"

He pointed a shaking paw.

It was snowing really heavily now. You couldn't even see the gates, let alone THE TRUNK with its ice bound passenger.

There was a pause. The mole stared at him. Then he opened his mouth and said again:

"*Yeeeeerrrsh?*"

Hamish could have wept with frustration. Did he have to do the whole speech again? It rather seemed that way.

"I need help!" he began again. "My name is Hamish Barleycorn and I'm - oh, look, never mind about all that. There's a world-famous-deep-frozen-history-expert out there! He urgently needs reheating"

The mole scratched his head, looking puzzled. It was becoming very clear to Hamish that he was not particularly quick on the uptake.

Best to keep it short and sweet.

"Frozen guinea pig!" bawled Hamish, pointing. "There! Quick! Fetch!"

That did the trick. Comprehension finally dawned in the mole's eyes.

Without a word, he handed Hamish the oil lamp, pushed past him, loped down the slippery steps three at a time and vanished into the whirling snow.

Hamish held his breath. Was the Professor all right? Could it be - the thought almost stopped his heart - could it be   possible that they were too late?

No.

"Dish one cold guinea pig."

The mole suddenly materialised out of the wild whiteness. Over his shoulder he carried the unyielding form of the Professor, who maintained the same frozen sitting posture. His legs were bent awkwardly at the knees. They protruded out in front, stiff as a board with Hamish's gravity-defying lunch box stuck firmly to his inverted lap. His head and shoulders stuck out behind at a right angle. The mole's huge, hairy arm was firmly clamped around his slippery middle. He rocked up and down like an oddly-shaped see- saw as his rescuer stomped briskly up the steps.

"Is he . . ?" whispered Hamish.

The mole regarded him gravely.

"Pig be all right. Thog make up fire. Get hot water. Hammer, chisel. Thog chip him.

Chip, chip, chip. Chip, chip, chip. Chip, chip, chip, chip, chip! He be all right."

Hamish breathed again.

CHAPTER FOUR

MOODY MUTTERINGS OF A MOLE IN LOVE

"ARE YOU SURE THERE'S NOTHING I CAN DO TO help?"

They stood in a vast, echoing room which was presumably the Great Hall. A long, polished table was set in the middle, directly beneath a huge crystal chandelier which hung suspended on a chain from the vaulted ceiling. At one end of the hall was a massive fireplace. The frozen Professor had been placed directly before it on a high backed chair. The mighty mole had taken what looked like half a tree trunk from the log pile and hurled it onto the glowing embers. The flames were now leaping and crackling nicely. Throughout the entire proceedings, he hadn't said a word.

Now, he looked up.

"Thog get shtuff from kitchen," he growled. "Hamshter shtay here."

"But can't I do something?" gibbered Hamish, hopping around in his anxiety. "Rub his paws? Breathe on him, or something?"

"No. Fire do work."

"But what about THE TRUNK? It's full of important equipment."

"Thog shee to luggage later. Firsht, deal with pig."

And with that, he shambled across to a low door set in the wall, ducking his head as he went through. Hamish heard his be-slippered feet descending what sounded like a flight of stone steps. They faded into the distance, and he was alone. Well, alone unless you counted the Professor, who right now wasn't exactly what you might call entertaining company.

He couldn't bear to look at him. So still and silent. So un-Professor-like. All that enthusiam stopped in its tracks. It was awful. He missed the Professor. He wanted him back, the way he was.

Well, perhaps just a *little* quieter.

To take his mind off the dreadfulness of

the situation, he began to look around.

The hall was a cavern of shadows. Candles set in niches cast their pale light on the suits of armour standing to rusty attention, their backs ramrod stiff against the stone walls.

At the opposite end to the fireplace, an imposing flight of steps led up to the minstrel gallery, which ran around all four corners of the hall. The walls were hung with crumbling, faded tapestries. and an impressive selection of ancient weapons - pikes, swords, cross bows, war hammers and those spikey things on the end of chains. Hamish wished he'd had one of those that time Stumpy McFeral pinched his new pen.

There were portraits too. Of long dead ancestors, Hamish supposed. The males wore long, flowing robes trimmed with what Hamish *hoped* was mock ermine. One or two were in armour. The females posed stiffly in a variety of fashionable dresses from different ages. Although painted by different artists and covering a wide period of history, all the subjects had one thing in common.

They were all rats. Brown rats, grey rats, white rats, black rats - all with the same sharp yellow teeth and the same pale, unfriendly eyes.

As he moved slowly around the hall, those cold eyes seemed to follow him. He could sense their disapproval.

There was a sudden, small noise in the silence. It came from the direction of the fire-place.

It was a drip!

Eagerly, Hamish ran back to the Professor. *Yesssss!* He punched his paw in the air. Things were looking up. The Professor was beginning to thaw, starting with the icicle hanging from the tip of his snout.

It was then that Hamish noticed the biggest, most impressive portrait of all hanging above the mantepiece.

A sleek white rat stared out from the ornate frame. He had the same pale eyes as the rest of the ancestral rats lining the walls.

He wore a long black cloak, lined with scarlet. He stood with one paw resting lightly on the shoulder of a seated female, who was dressed in a simple, white, flowing gown. Her fur was not so much white as silvery. She looked very young.

And beautiful, Hamish mentally added.

"Dat Mashter," rasped a voice from just behind him. "An 'dat My Lady."

Hamish whirled round. Thog stood directly behind him, holding a large bucket of steaming water in one hand and a tool bag in the other.

"Golly!" said Hamish, all of a do. "You scared me then!"

The mole took no notice. He was staring up at the portrait with a rapt expression on his face.

"Dat My Lady," he said again. He set down the tool bag and pointed. "Dat Rodentia. She neesh."

There was something about the way that he said the name. The pride. The awe. The longing. There was no doubt about it. Thog was in love.

"You're right," said Hamish. "She does

look nice. Nice dress."

"Not nishe! Neesh! Neesh! She Mashter'sh *neesh*!" He was terribly agitated. The water slopped about in the bucket.

"Oh, I *see!* She's his *niece*! Right. At any rate, she's very pretty."

Thog tore his eyes away from the portrait and looked down at Hamish with a pitying expression.

"She not pretty," he said, in terrible tones. "She *bootiful*!"

"Yes," said Hamish, nodding away like an idiot. "That's what I meant."

"You mean," said Thog, looking at him hard. "You mean you *like* her?"

Hamish felt himself on dangerous ground. "No. Yes. No. Yes, I mean."

Whichever he said seemed to be wrong. He attempted a light little laugh and changed the subject.

"And where is your master now?" he enquired. "All tucked up in bed, I suppose?"

A crafty expression crept over the mole's coarse features.

"Out," he said briefly.

"Out? It's rather late to be out."

"Mashter wait for visitorsh. Visitorsh no come. Mashter hungry. Go out for dinner. Back late. Very, very late. You shee him tomorrow."

There was a sharp, tinkling noise behind them. The icicle had fallen from the Professor's snout. A small puddle was forming around his feet.

"Thog chip pig now," said the mole, and bent over his tool bag. From it, he withdrew a large mallet and a wickedly sharp looking chisel.

Hamish looked around. Chipping the

Professor free was, he suspected, going to be a long job. He saw a small footstool on the far side of the hall and went to fetch it.

When he got back, Thog was hard at work on the Professor's left cheek. Bang, bang, bang, went the hammer on the chisel. Little splinters of ice fell tinkling to the stone floor. It was horrible to watch. Hamish's eyes lifted again to the portrait above the mantle.

"I didn't know His Excellency had a niece," he remarked conversationally. "Is she visiting, or something?"

"No. She live here. Mashter take care of her. And Thog. Thog take *good* care of her. And she take good care of Thog. She give Thog nishe things. Presentsh."

"Really? Like what?"

"Like - theshe slippersh!" He indicated the pink fluffy creations adorning his feet with pride.

"Lovely," said Hamish. "They obviously mean a great deal to you."

Privately, he thought the brown zippered variety would have been more suitable. Still, it was the thought that counted. It was clear that the Count's niece had a kind heart.

"How long do you think this will take?" he enquired, giving a little yawn. The heat from the blazing fire was making him sleepy. He noticed that he was beginning to steam as the warmth from the roaring fire finally began to permeate his soaked clothing.

"Long job. You want go bed?"

"Oh, no. No, I must stay here. I want to be at the Professor's side when he comes to. He'll be weak and confused. He'll need me."

Thog wasn't listening. He was working away at getting the Professor' s frozen hat loose and muttering *chip, chip, chip*, to himself in a droning undertone.

And that was the last thing Hamish heard that night.

CHAPTER FIVE

A MEAL, A MOUSE AND A MYSTERIOUS MESSAGE

"AH HA! HAMISH! ZERE YOU ARE, MY LITTLE friend! All bright-eyed and bushy-tailed after a goot night's sleep, eh? Oh! I forgot! You don't haff a bushy tail, ha ha!"

The Professor sat slap bang in the middle of the long table. Before him was a huge bowl of cereal, a steaming mug of tea and a plateful of toast crumbs. From the state of his whiskers, it appeared he had been tucking in for some time. Weak and confused he wasn't.

"Professor!" gasped Hamish, hurrying down the last of the stone steps. "You're all right! Oh, thank goodness for that!"

"Right? Of course I am all right. Never better. Zis kindly mole see to zat."

65

He waved his spoon in the direction of the fireplace. A fire still burned there - not as fiercely as the previous night, but brightly enough to take the chill from the vast hall.

Thog was bent over the wood pile, hairy arms adding more freshly cut logs.

"Thanks for carrying me up to my room last night," Hamish called. "It *was* you, wasn't it?"

Thog said nothing. He straightened, brushed bark-dust from his paws and shambled off through the kitchen doorway. Hamish noticed that he wasn't wearing his lovely pink slippers this morning. Instead, he was sporting a pair of huge, steel-capped boots, which laced up to mid-shin. They were the sort of boots that could kick holes in an armoured tank. On the whole, Hamish preferred the slippers.

"I dropped off, I'm afraid," said Hamish, rather guiltily. "I'm terribly sorry. I wanted to be there when you - um - emerged - but I was so tired, what with the journey and everything . . . ."

"Sink nussing of it!" cried the Professor, patting at his whiskers with a napkin. "You did your bit, Hamish. Vot more can I ask? Anyvay, I voz in capable paws. Now, tell me. How do you find your room?"

"Well, it's a bit complicated. I think it's up the steps, turn left along the minstrel gallery, through another doorway, along a corridor . . ."

"Nein, nein! I mean, how do you *find* it ? Is it to your liking?"

"Oh, I *see*." Hamish thought about this. For preference, he liked a cosy room. A snug room, with glowing side lamps and jolly pictures and thick rugs. A room with a soft, warm bed and a straw-stuffed mattress you could lose yourself in. A Hamster-ish room.

The room he had woken up in that morning wasn't exactly cosy. The mattress he lay on felt as though it was stuffed with barbed wire, and the rug covering him was unpleasantly scratchy and barely adequate against the bitter cold. If it wasn't for the fact that he was still wearing his clothes, he would most probably have frozen to death in his sleep.

There was nothing much in the way of furnishings either. Just a narrow bed, a rough stool, a large chest of drawers, a small table containing a single candlestick, a jug of icy water to wash with and a row of pegs hammered into the panelled walls. His backpack hung on one of the pegs, his umbrella was hooked over another, his scarf was neatly placed on a third and his lunchbox hung from a fourth.

When he shivered over to the window and pulled back the thick, dusty curtain, he found that it overlooked a sunken garden filled with crumbly statues. An iced-over fountain stood in the middle. The garden was enclosed by tall, ivy covered stone walls. A small gate was set in the far wall. Beyond the walled garden lay a jumble of outbuildings, outlined starkly against the white of the snow - and beyond those lay the dark forest. It was a chilly view.

"It's nice," said Hamish. He didn't wish to appear negative at this early stage in the proceedings.

"Excellent! Mine too is most satisfactory. Vun thing, it has zis curious little door set in ze vall . . . ah, Gretchen! Zere you are, my dear."

Hamish looked up in surprise. Approaching the table with a tray in her paws was the small grey mouse from the inn!

"You remember young Gretchen, Hamish," cried the Professor, giving him a knowing wink. "Our little friend from last night!"

"Hello," said Hamish, rather more gruffly than he intended.

"Hello," said Gretchen. "I've done you some eggs."

She set the tray on the table and took from it a dish containing scrambled eggs. They were light and fluffy, just how Hamish liked them.

There was a glass of carrot juice too - and a plateful of buttered toast. Suddenly, he realised he was starving. The half roll he had carried in his cheek pouch was long gone. He had swallowed it by mistake the night before, when the fortune-telling squirrel had grabbed hold of his coat sleeve.

"Gretchen comes up here to help out ven ze Count has ze visitors," explained the Professor. "She cook ze breakfast and deal viz ze laundry. Ve haff been haffing nice little chat, haven't ve, dear?

"We certainly have," said Gretchen. "The Professor's been telling me all about you, Hamish. I hear you're a bit of a hero. You saved his life last night."

"Well I don't know about that . . ." mumbled Hamish modestly. He blushed and looked down, making a mental note not to carry around his lunchbox in her presence. It wasn't the sort of thing heroes should be seen with.

Just then, there came a noise from the kitchen doorway. Thog had returned, with another armful of logs. He was giving Gretchen what looked like a warning glare. She returned it with a brief, rather cocky glance, then turned her attention back to the Professor.

"Any more cereal, Professor?"

"No, no, three bowls is sufficient. Of course, if zere should be a *leetle* bit more of zat fried chickveed hanging about . . . ?"

"Of course. I'll get it right away."

And off she tripped, tray in hand, tail held perkily behind.

"Loffly girl," said the Professor. "My, zose eggs look delicious, Hamish. May I?"

"Er . . ."

The Professor pulled the plate towards him and scooped up a large forkful.

"Ve must eat goot breakfast, for today, ve explore! My friend Sog here tells me our host is still abed. Isn't zat right, Sog?"

"Mashter shleep now," agreed Thog. "Get up later."

"Fine, fine! So ve are left to our own devices for now, Hamish. My, zese eggs are

71

goot! First, I unpack my books, get my notes, my pencil, my tape measure, all ze sings I need. Zen ve go out and exlore ze grounds, jah?"

"Oh, really?" Hamish tried not to sound too doleful. The snow had finally stopped, but it still looked darned cold out there. "Don't you think perhaps you should stay inside today? After what happened to you last night?" he added hopefully.

"Stay in? Stay in? Vild foxes vouldn't keep me in. No, a good stiff valk around ze grounds is vot ve need. Ve must take ze opportunity, now ze snow has stopped."

"Yes. Right. Of course."

Hamish felt guilty. If the Professor felt up to a morning of tramping around the grounds after his shocking experience, who was he to act all wimpy?

He watched sorrowfully as the last of his eggs disappeared down the Professor's throat.

"Oh yes, ve haff much vork to do. Ve make notes, drawings, take measurements! Ve haff to make a map! Zere is no time to lose."

Absent mindedly, he began on Hamish's toast.

"Um . . ." said Hamish, reaching out hopefully. But he was too late.

"Look! Look over zere! Vot treasures surround us! If zat is not a rare example of an early Fourteenth-century urn, I vill eat my hat . . ."

The Professor shot from his seat and rushed away to examine a large, chipped, cobwebby pot, taking the plate of toast with him.

He might as well eat his hat, reflected Hamish ruefully. He's demolished everything else in sight. Apart from the carrot juice.

He was just about to reach for his glass when Gretchen returned from the kitchen with the Professor's fried chickweed.

"Here we are, Professor," she said brightly. "Get stuck into that."

"Chick veed, chick veed, how I loff ze chick veed!"

The Professor scurried back to his seat with alacrity. "Um um! Zis is delicious, my dear, simply delicious! Zis mouse can cook, Hamish. I tell you zat."

"I'm sure she can," said Hamish wistfully, as Gretchen cleared away his empty plate.

The Professor shovelled in the last crunchy mouthful, reached for Hamish's carrot juice, downed it in one and shot to his feet, rubbing his paws together in anticipation of the delights to come.

"Vell," he said. "if you vill excuse me, I must prepare. Hamish, ve vill meet by ze main door in vun half hour precisely. I suggest you vear your scarf. You know, I promised your dear muzzer I vould make sure zat . . ."

"Fine, fine!" broke in Hamish hastily. "Don't you worry, Professor. I'll be ready."

The Professor stumped off up the great stairway, humming as he went. Hamish was left behind, feeling very hungry but trying not to mind too much.

"Thog," said Gretchen suddenly. "I thought I saw someone in the grounds just now. Outside the kitchen window."

"Uh?"

"I said, I thought I saw someone outside.

74

I may have been mistaken, but perhaps you should go and check?"

"Uh?"

"Stranger! Outside! Find!"

That did it. In seconds, the gigantic mole was nowhere to be seen.

Then, something rather strange happened. The moment he was out of sight, Gretchen scrabbled wildly in her apron pocket and produced a small piece of folded paper.

"Here," she hissed, thrusting it at Hamish.

"What . . ?"

"Don't say a word. Put it somewhere safe. Wait until you're alone, then read it, all right?"

"Well - all right, but what . . ?"

"Ssssh. The walls have ears. I've got to go."

And she snatched up the tray, tripped lightly across to the kitchen doorway and vanished, without a backward glance.

Hamish stared down at the note in his paw. Then he looked at the walls. They didn't have ears, that was for sure - but they certainly had eyes. Dozens of them. Hard, pale eyes, staring down at him accusingly.

Automatically, he stuffed the note into his cheek pouch.

Nobody would look for it there. Or if they did, they'd have to get past his teeth first!

It took him some time to find his room again. The castle was a warren of passages and confusing flights of steps. He kept arriving at dead ends and locked doors. However, at last he saw a door he thought he recognised, and flung it open.

Sure enough, there was his backpack and his scarf and his own dear lunchbox. Eagerly, he hurried across to the bed, sat down and removed the piece of folded paper from his pouch.

Paws shaking slightly with excitement, he unfolded it. It was brief and to the point.

Dear Hamish,
I must speak to you in private. You are in grave danger. Meet me after breakfast tomorrow in the walled garden, and I will explain everything. Above all, make sure you carry the garlic with you. AT ALL TIMES!

Gretchen

P.S. Be sure to lock your door at night.

P.P.S. Do not mention this note to anybody. Destroy it when you've read it.

"Golly," said Hamish, with a little gulp.

He read it through once again, then folded it up, placed it in his mouth and swallowed.

Crazy old toothsayers, gates that opened by themselves, monster moles in pink slippers, mysterious warning notes. Whatever next?

CHAPTER SIX

SALT, SWEET SMILES AND A SLUG IN THE SALAD

THERE WAS NO STOPPING THE PROFESSOR. HIS chilly experience of the night before seemed to have given him even more energy, if that was possible. All day long he tramped about the snow covered castle grounds, taking notes, measuring, estimating and falling upon each new mossy gargoyle or crumbling statue with cries of wonder and delight.

Hamish did all the donkey work. He toiled around behind, carrying the equipment - reference books, mainly, plus a funny little box on a tripod which came with a black cloth, under which the Professor would duck from time to time.

He teetered along high walls in order to check the length of a gargoyle's nose. He counted the number of steps on innumerable flights by plodding up and down them. Sometimes he tripped, lost count and had to do it twice. He edged along precarious ledges in order to measure the dimensions of particularly interesting windows. And when he wasn't risking life and limb, he sharpened pencils and looked things up in reference books until his brain was reeling.

Gretchen had provided them both with a packed lunch, which the Professor had taken charge of. Hamish was looking forward to his tremendously. After all, not a morsel had passed his lips that day, apart from the mysterious note, which was hardly filling.

At midday, he plodded down a particularly high flight of steps to find the Professor perched at the bottom, tidily folding up a piece of greaseproof paper.

"Ah," said Hamish, sitting down next to him. "Lunch. My, I'm looking forward to this."

"So you should. Eat, my boy. You haff vorked hard."

There was a little pause.

"Can I have it, then, please?" asked Hamish.

"Vot? But you haff it in your pocket."

"No I don't. She gave them both to you, remember?"

A guilty look came over the Professor's face.

80

"Oh," he said. "Vos zat meant for both of us? I am so sorry, Hamish. How silly of me."

"That's all right," said Hamish, nobly. "It's an easy mistake to make."

Nevertheless, he couldn't help feeling just a bit hard done by. It seemed he was destined never to eat on this expedition, whereas the Professor seemed to do little else

"Cheer up," said the Professor, catching his woebegone expression. " You vill make up for it at dinner, eh? Now. To vork. Could you just pop up to ze top of zat tower over zere and climb onto ze roof and do a little sketch of zat vezzer vane? I'd do it myself, but I haff a slight touch of indigestion."

The day wore on. The mysterious note from Gretchen was very much on Hamish's mind. Several times he found himself on the verge of mentioning it to the Professor - but managed to stop himself. She had, after all, asked him to say nothing. Besides, the Professor was having such a wonderful time, he doubted whether he would even take it in. What were mysterious notes compared with the delights of an unexplored castle?

"Look, Hamish!" he would cry. "A

perfect example of ze medieval vatch tower! See how ze fontenels are placed at ze exact angle to accomodate ze grommited funiculees, vich in turn support ze funiculas!"

Or something like that.

Throughout the entire day, they saw no sign of their host. In fact, they saw no one at all apart from Thog - and even he stayed in the background. They kept catching glimpses of him, dragging great bundles of firewood in from the forest and stacking them in one of the outbuildings. Occasionally, Hamish would glimpse him standing motionless behind a headless statue or sagging pillar, huge arms hanging almost to the ground. Hamish kept giving him friendly little waves, which were not returned. He had a feeling Thog was keeping an eye on them.

Dusk was falling when the Professor finally decided to call it a day.

"A great day's vork, eh, Hamish?" he was exclaiming as they walked down the long, echoing corridor that led to the Great Hall. "Tomorrow, I write up all my notes. I am hoping His Excellency vill allow me to use ze library. Zere is sure to be a library, probably stuffed to ze rafters viz rare books and manuscripts. I can't vait to get my paws on zem. Books, books, how I loff . . ."

He broke off. They had reached the entrance to the Hall. A hundred candles flickered in the chandelier hanging above the great table. The fire blazed in the hearth. Standing before it, one paw resting lightly on the mantelpiece, stood the rat in the picture.

White, he was. So very, very white.

He was also tall, thin and elegant. He wore the same floor length black cloak as in the portrait. His long, scaley, muscular tail protruded below, arranged in neat coils. His sleek head was bowed as he stared broodingly down into the flames, sipping from a glass containing what looked like red wine.

He looked up sharply at the sound of their entrance. Then, he set down his wine glass on the mantelpiece and smiled. It was a full, welcoming smile. Though it contained a lot of sharp, white teeth, and didn't quite seem to reach his eyes.

"Ahh," he said. His voice was low and pleasant. "My dear Professor! We meet at last. Welcome. I am Ratula."

He held out a thin, white paw.

"Your Excellency!" burst out the Professor, hurrying forwards, dropping his notebook in his excitement. "So long I haff been vaiting to make your aqvaintance! Such an honour, sir, such an honour!"

He grasped the rat's paw in his own and pumped it up and down.

"My apologies for not being here to greet you on your arrival. I trust Thog has been looking after you?" enquired the Count, still smiling.

"Indeed he has, sir, indeed he has."

"Good. He told me of your distressing experience last night. I hope you are fully recovered?"

"I am as recovered as recycled old sofa! Good as new. Better, in fact."

"Excellent." The Count turned to look at Hamish, who stood hesitating in the doorway with his arms full of equipment. "And this, I take it, is your young assistant?"

"Yes, yes, zat is Hamish. Come, Hamish, come and shake hands viz our host!"

Hamish set down the books, the notepads and the funny box on the tripod and walked forward.

The Count's eyes swept over him. as he approached. For some reason, Hamish found it hard to meet those strange, washed out, colourless eyes.

"Hamish," said Ratula in his low, melodious voice. "How *very* nice to meet you."

He really sounded as though he meant it. Hamish found he liked him. So what if he had funny eyes? Lots of animals had funny eyes. Mrs Golightly had funny eyes, he remembered. They were so crossed that two animals answered every time she asked a question. That didn't mean she wasn't nice underneath.

Shyly, he reached up and took the pro-ferred paw.

It was cold! Terribly cold. He could feel it, even through his mittens. It was a bit like holding a fish straight off its bed of ice on the fishmonger's barrow. The Count must suffer from very poor circulation.

Hamish tried to withdraw his paw, and found he couldn't. Ratula held it in his icy grip, still smiling away. Hamish pulled a little harder. He didn't want to be impolite, but his paw was beginning to go numb. At last, to his relief, the Count released it.

"Now," he said briskly. "You will no doubt be hungry?"

"Vell, I confess I am, a little," said the Professor. "You, Hamish?"

"Starving," agreed Hamish, who was.

"Good. Thog has prepared dinner. Perhaps you would like to wash and change? Tonight, we dine early. At nine."

"Excellent, excellent! And I must confess, dear Count, I vos rozzer hoping zat you might give us a guided tour of zis oh so vonderful castle ?"

"To be sure. Directly we have eaten. Until nine, then."

And he gave them one last, charming smile, lowered his head once again and looked into the flames.

It rather seemed as though they were dismissed.

At nine o'clock precisely, they took their places at the table. The Count sat on a high backed chair at one end. Hamish, wearing his better shirt and the Professor, who only seemed to have the one outfit, sat opposite each other in the middle. The chair at the far end remained empty.

The table was laid with polished silver-ware and long stemmed glasses. Hamish looked down at the bewildering array of cutlery arranged before him with an anxious little frown. He was trying to remember what his mum had told him. Did you work from the outside in, or inside out? He was attempting to puzzle it out, when:

"Ah Rodentia, my dear," said the Count, pushing back his chair and standing. "Come. Allow me to introduce our guests. Professor Von Strudel, Hamish - meet Rodentia, my niece."

Hamish looked up. Standing poised at the top of the flight of steps stood the young rat from the portrait.

She was even more beautiful in the flesh. Her silvery fur shimmered like silk. Her whiskers were the longest Hamish had ever seen. She began to descend the stairway, daintily holding up the hem of her long white gown. Her slim tail trailed behind her, like a bride's train.

Both the Professor and Hamish shot hastily to their feet.

Smiling, she approached the table and dropped a demure curtesy.

"Good evening, Uncle. Have you been waiting long? I'm afraid I got quite carried away with my embroidery. How do you do, Professor, Hamish? I am so pleased to meet you."

Her voice was like the tinkle of tiny silver bells. Light, sweet and fragile. Hamish bowed low. When he came up again, he saw that he was the only one left standing so he sat down hastily, trying to wipe the soppy grin from his face.

"So," said Ratula, taking a folded napkin and spreading it out on his lap. "We are all here. Let us eat."

Thog appeared on cue, pushing before him a squealing trolley on which stood a vast, silver domed platter and several other dishes containing fruits and cheeses. Tonight, he was dressed in an ancient frock coat which strained across his huge shoulders. Hamish glanced at his feet. No pink slippers. No big boots either. Instead, he wore a pair of polished black shoes, which squeaked as he walked.

He wheeled the trolley to the Count's end of the table and raised the lid of the platter, revealing a veritable feast of braised nuts, steamed vegetables and heaped piles of grain.

"Mashter?" he enquired.

"I thank you, no," said the Count smoothly. "I fear I have a poor appetite," he added to the Professor, by way of explanation. "I suffer an allergic reaction to many foods. I find that a light, liquid diet suits me best. But do, please, go ahead."

The Professor didn't need any encouragement.

When it was Rodentia's turn to be served, she had a very frugal portion. Hamish noticed that the great mole's paw trembled a little as he placed a plate before her. She looked up and smiled gently at him.

"Thank you, Thog," she said in her sweet, musical voice. "You've really outdone yourself this time. It looks wonderful."

The huge mole hung his head and shuffled back to the trolley. He took a large, dirty rag from his pocket and blew his nose loudly before dealing with Hamish's plate. He took his time. Hamish forced himself to look away. He was so hungry, he was beginning to drool.

At the far end of the table, the Count and the Professor were heavily involved in intelligent conversation about the castle. Right now, they were knee deep in flying buttresses, abutments, retaining walls, Gothic arches and such like. The Professor was also managing to shovel in plenty of dinner, Hamish noticed. The Count seemed content to sip at his glass of red wine.

Hamish cast a shy little glance at Rodentia as she played with the small portion on her plate. She was so beautiful, she made him tongue tied. He wanted to talk to her, but didn't know how to begin. Suddenly, the problem was solved. She turned to him, made a little face and whispered: "It's awfully complicated, isn't it? What they're talking about. I only understand about one word in ten. Of course, I suppose that's just me being silly. I expect you understand it all, being the Professor's assistant?"

"Oh, no," Hamish hastened to reassure her. Had he been the world's expert on flying buttresses, he wouldn't have admitted it. If

Rodentia thought she was silly, he was darned sure he was going to be sillier. "I don't understand it either. I'm new to all this, you see."

"Really? You must tell me all about yourself. It must be so interesting, being apprenticed to someone so clever."

"Oh, it is. But I'm not brainy at all. I just carry things about and hold stuff. You wouldn't want to hear about me."

"Yes I do. I want to hear everything."

THWACK!

Hamish's dinner thumped under his nose. Pleased though he was to be talking to the beautiful Rodentia, he couldn't contain his hunger any more. Ravenous, he picked up the nearest fork and dug in.

Salt! The bitter, overwhelming taste of it flooded his mouth. Thog must have emptied the entire contents of the salt cellar in there. His mouth puckered up like a concertina, and he hastily reached for his napkin. He pushed the plate away, turned from the table, eyes watering, and furtively spat the disgusting mouthful into a fold of the cloth. In doing so, he caught Thog's eye. Thog leered.

"What's the matter?" asked Rodentia. "Don't you like your food?"

"It's - er - just a touch too salty for me, actually . . ." gasped Hamish, reaching for the water jug.

"Thog, our guest's food isn't to his taste. Remove his plate and serve him with some salad, would you?"

"Right away, My Lady."

Thog creaked off to do as he was told.

"So, tell me," continued Rodentia, placing her perfect chin in her paws and gazing at him through her long, sweeping eyelashes. "Do you like music, Hamish?"

"Oh, I do," nodded Hamish, who was tone deaf.

"Me too. What's your favourite kind?"

"The Diggory Dormice," said Hamish, in between chucking glass after glass of water down his throat. They were, without doubt, his favourite group.

"I don't think I've heard of them," said Rodentia, thoughtfully.

Hamish was amazed. He thought everyone in the world had heard of the Diggs, as their fans called them.

"What about your hobbies?" enquired Rodentia.

Hamish thought. What were his hobbies?

"Well, I used to play quite a lot of football. And I kept an ant farm once. Had to give it up, though. The poor little things kept falling off the tractor." He smiled hopefully.

Rodentia stared at him with wide eyes. Then, she broke into peals of tinkling laughter.

"Oh! That is a joke, is it not? I have never heard a joke before. Oh, how funny you are, Hamish!"

Hamish goggled at her in amazement. Never heard a joke before? Never heard of the Diggs? What a strange life she must lead.

"What about you?" he asked. "Do you have any hobbies?"

"Embroidery," said Rodentia promptly. "And I play the harp."

She would, thought Hamish. A harp. Wasn't that what angels played?

"I read a lot too," she continued. "Do you?"

"Oh, yes. Loads."

"What's your favourite book?"

"*Three Stoats in a Boat*," said Hamish. Actually, he had never managed to get past chapter two, but he didn't mention that.

"I like romantic novels," confessed Rodentia. "Ones where the hero carries the heroine off into the sunset." She gave a little sigh, pushed her food around her plate, then looked up brightly. "Don't you?" she added.

"Oh, yes," lied Hamish, who preferred football magazines. "Nothing like a bit of romance, I always say. Love makes the world go rou–"

THWACK!

A plate of salad came smashing down before him with such force that a radish flipped up and hit him in the eye before rolling off under the table. He looked up, startled. Thog stood at his shoulder, breathing deeply. His huge, shovel like paws were flexing and a low, warning rumble was sounding deep within his chest.

Hamish looked at the salad. It was a nice looking salad. The lettuce was green and crisp. The cucumber was arranged tastifully in thin slices around the edge. The radishes were round and red. The tomato in the middle looked temptingly juicy. Or it would have done if it hadn't been for the small, plump slug artistically placed on top.

Hamish looked at the slug.

The slug looked back at Hamish and waved its tiny eye stalks in a cheery fashion.

Then Hamish met Thog's small, hot little eyes. Jealousy kindled there. Mad, white-hot jealousy. He pushed the plate of salad to one side.

Some time later, as Thog cleared the plates away, the Count stood up.

"So, my friends. Are you ready? Shall we proceed?"

"Ready?" cried the Professor, bouncing

to his feet with alacrity. "Ve haff been vaiting for zis moment viz ze bated breath. Isn't zat so, Hamish?"

"Oh, yes," said Hamish, who had indeed been looking forward to it. The trouble was, he was ravenous. He just hoped he'd have the strength to stand.

"Good. And you, my dear? Will you join us?"

To Hamish's disappointment, Rodentia shook her head.

"No, uncle. If you will excuse me, I'm feeling rather tired."

"Of course. You must forgive her, Professor. We are unused to all this socialising. We lead a quiet life as a rule, do we not, Rodentia?"

"Indeed we do."

She sounded a little sad, Hamish thought.

All eyes were on her as she dropped a curtesy and glided away towards the stairway. Thog stood at the bottom and stretched out a helping paw as she set a dainty foot on the first step. She stopped and gently patted his shoulder before moving on up.

Thog gazed adoringly after her retreating form.

How kind she is, thought Hamish.

CHAPTER SEVEN

A TIRING TOUR AND A CHARGING CHEST

"AND LASTLY, WE HAVE THE KITCHEN," announced the Count, leading them down a flight of steps into a large, echoing cavern of a place, with flagstoned floors and beams hung with bunches of dried herbs. Pots, pans and carving knives hung from hooks on the walls. At one end was a large black range. Thog stood at a deep sink, up to his elbows in greasy water. The slippers were back on and he wore a pink frilled apron over his butler's suit. Another present from Rodentia, by the looks of it.

Hamish was tired. He leaned against the wall and suppressed a yawn. The tour of the castle had indeed been interesting, but the combination of cold and hunger was finally beginning to have an effect. He wished he had thought to put his coat on, but it was hanging on a hook by the front door and he hadn't liked to hold things up while he went to get it.

For the last hour, they had followed the Count along what seemed like miles of dimly lit corridors and up and down interminable flights of steps. The Professor was, as always, bursting with enthusiam, asking question after question and only pausing to scribble in his rapidly filling notebook. They had peered into dozens of dark, silent rooms, where the furniture was draped with ghostly dust sheets. They had visited the armoury (piles of rusty weapons and ancient battle gear). They had ducked under a low arch-way, climbed yet another flight of steps and stepped out onto the snow covered battle-ments, where they stood in a bone-freezing wind admiring the moon through chattering teeth until the Professor' s hat blew away and they had to come in. The Count didn't seem to notice the cold. In fact, standing on the ramparts with his black cloak streaming behind him and his sharp nose sniffing the arctic wind, he seemed to relish it.

A Tiring Tour and a Charging Chest

Next came the library, which had sent the Professor into a state of gibbering delerium, with its oak panelled walls and shelf after shelf of dusty books and cabinets crammed with rare, yellowing manuscripts.

"But zis is marvelous!" the Professor had squawked, scuttling between the shelves and peering delightedly at the faded titles. " You haff ze first edition of *Ze Rise and Fall of Ze Gerbil Empire!* And, look! *A Complete History of ze Fruit Bat,* by my old friend and colleague Professor Frank le Barkin. And, see here! Ze seminal *Life Cycle Of Ze House Flea* by Constance Scratchin. And, oh! Ze entire series of *Goosepimples*! All ze major vorks are here! Oh, zis is too much!"

"Do, please, feel free to use it whenever you wish," said the Count, with a little smile. "There is a writing desk over in the corner. I will instruct Thog to furnish you with pen and ink."

It had been hard to drag the Professor away from the library. It was, as far as he was concerned, the high spot of the guided tour. Hamish, however, was beginning to flag. Privately, he was more than relieved when the Count announced that the kitchen would be their last port of call.

Not so the Professor. He never seemed to run out of steam.

"Ah!" he cried, twirling around in the middle of the floor, his eyes taking in every detail. "So, zis is vere it all happens! Fascinating, fascinating. And zis little door over here. Vere does zis lead?"

He scuttled towards a stout wooden door set into the wall. But his way was blocked. With a speed incredible to one of his bulk, Thog got there first. With a low growl, he hurled himself across the kitchen. He stood in a low, wrestling style crouch, knuckles brushing the floor, breathing heavily, holding a dripping dishmop in his soapy fist in an altogether threatening way.

"The vaults," said Ratula, briefly.

"Really? May ve see?"

"Sadly, I'm afraid not. It's too dangerous. The roof is no longer stable. There have been one or two falls. That's why the door is locked. Only Thog has the key. He has instructions to let no one in. All right, Thog. Back! Down, I say!"

Obediently, the great mole bowed his head and slunk off back to his sink.

"And there, I'm afraid, the tour must end," concluded the Count smoothly. "The hour is late. Young Hamish looks as though he is ready to drop."

"Of course, of course. How selfish of me. I forget ze boy is only a youngster."

The three of them climbed back up the winding stairway and re-emerged into the Great Hall.

"I shall bid you goodnight, then," said Ratula. "Until tomorrow."

"Gootnight, Excellency. I sank you for your vunderful hospitality," cried the Professor, beginning to make his way up the stairs. "Come, Hamish. Let us away to our beds."

"I'll be up in a minute," said Hamish, yawning. "I just want to collect something."

And he hurried from the Hall and along the corridor to the front door, where his coat hung with the head of garlic in the pocket.

When he got back, the Great Hall was empty. The only light came from the glowing embers of the dying fire. He stood for a moment, staring around into the darkness. He couldn't see a thing. Except for . . .

Eyes. The eyes in the ancestral portraits lining the walls.

They appeared to be glowing! Little pin-pricks of light, staring down at him.

With a gulp, he wrapped his coat around himself, scuttled across the vast wilderness of the floor and fled up the stairs.

His bedroom was as cold as ever. Somebody - Thog, presumably - had drawn the heavy curtains across the window and placed a fresh candle on the bedside table.

Breath freezing in the chill air, Hamish rummaged through his backpack and found the new pyjamas his Auntie Enid had given him for Christmas. It was a pity about the design (red fire engines, no less! Was there no end to his relations' ability to humiliate him?) but at least they were warm. In record time he removed his clothes, climbed into the embarrassing pyjamas, broke the ice on the water jug with his toothbrush, swilled freezing water around his chattering teeth, spead his coat on the bed for extra warmth and climbed in.

Sprong! went the springs as he snuggled down.

He lay on his back, unwilling to snuff out the candle just yet. Tired though he was, his brain didn't seem to want to slow down. He couldn't stop thinking about Gretchen's mysterious note.

You are in grave danger. Whatever could

she mean? He had had one or two small accidents that day to be sure, but at no time had he been in any *real* danger. Unless you counted the danger of starving to death, but he didn't think she meant that.

Or could it be that she believed the castle to be haunted? Hamish gave a slightly superior little smile. That was probably it. As the Professor had remarked, these simple country folk tended to be superstitious.

Or, perhaps she meant that he was in danger from Thog? Surely not. He wasn't keen on Hamish muscling in on his lady love, and he liked to be taken seriously in his job as chief of security - but was he *really* dangerous?

There was something else he didn't understand. Why was she making such a fuss about the garlic?

Was Thog likely come bursting in armed with a banjo and give him a quick burst of *One Mole Went To Mow* before hitting him over the head with a washing up mop, or something?

Still. It seemed important to her, so he supposed he' d better do it. With a little sigh, he threw back the covers and pattered across the cold floor to the door.

There was no key.

That was that, then. At least he'd tried. Shivering, he scurried back to bed and slipped under the rug. He was about to blow out the candle, when he heard a noise. A scraping, grinding noise. Startled, he looked across the room to the large chest of drawers which stood in deep shadow against the far wall.

Was it his imagination?

No. There was no doubt about it.

The chest was moving! Slowly, menacingly, it was trundling forward away from the wall and relentlessly advancing towards him across the room!

He opened his mouth to squeak - but nothing came out. Eyes bulging, he watched the large piece of furniture bearing down on him; a grim nightmare of creaking joints, rattling drawers and squealing castors.

Then, just as he was about to leap from his bed and get out of its path - it stopped. Behind it, a section of the panelled wall opened up, and light spilled into the room. Standing in the space where the panel had been, was a portly figure, clad in a white nightshirt and stripey nightcap with a little bobble on the end.

"Aha!" rang out the all too familiar tones. "So *zis* is vere ze mysterious little door leads to!"

"Professor!" gasped Hamish weakly, as his fluttering heart stopped tap-dancing in his chest and settled back to the dull but vital task of pushing blood around his body. "I wasn't expecting you."

"Isn't zis nice? Ve are next door to each uzzer. I didn't realize zat, did you?"

"No. I didn't."

"Zis is most convenient. If ve get lonely

in ze night, ve can shout to each uzzer, jah?"

"Mmmm."

"Or maybe ve vill sing duets!"

"Er - sing *duets*? In the *night*?"

"Is habit, you know?" The Professor gave a rueful little chuckle. "If I cannot sleep, I sing. Songs from ze old country, mainly. Little songs my nanny teach me. Of course, I do ze more popular stuff too. Is my vay of relaxing. Do you haff any reqvests? I can do most styles."

"No. Not that I can think of right now."

"Oh vell. I leave you to sleep, zen. Gootnight, Hamish."

"Goodnight, Professor."

The Professor tiptoed back into his own room, pulling the panelled door shut behind him with a thoughtful crash.

Hamish stared at the door. He hadn't even noticed it. It blended in perfectly with the panelling. Funny idea to put a chest of drawers in front of it.

In a way, it was comforting to know that the Professor was next door.

On the other hand . . . that business about singing . . .

A fraction of a second later, his worst fears were realised.

"*Gerbils in ze night, exchanging glances,*" came the sounds of a rich baritone from next door.

Hamish blew out the candle.

"*Gerbils in ze night, all doing dances . . .*"

Oh no. He was of those singers who never got the words right. Hamish lay down and pulled the rug up over his ears.

"*Dooby dooby dooo . . .*"

Hamish pulled the pillow over his head., and tried to get to sleep.

One rendition of *Gerbils in the Night,* one of *Ze Big Sheep Sails on ze Allyallyoop* and one very long, emotional *Oh, My Loff is Like a Red, Red Radish* later, he succeeded.

CHAPTER EIGHT

A SAD SONG AND A SEARCH FOR THE SINGER

IT WAS SINGING THAT WOKE HIM. NOT THE Professor's singing, though. This singing was very different.

It was sweet, pure and faraway. The silvery tones drifted along the corridors and down the echoing stairwells, hauntingly beautiful.

He sat up in bed, ears erect. How long had he been asleep? There was no telling what the time was. For the umpteenth time, he wished he had a watch. He'd had one once, but Stumpy McFeral had taken it apart with his boot one wet playtime. Hamish had begged his mum for another one for his birthday, but had been briskly reminded that he hadn't looked after the first one

111

properly and been given a Junior Carpentry set instead.

There was silence from the room next door. The Professor had evidently run out of musical steam. Just as well. It would have been a crime to drown out the dulcet tones which wafted towards him now.

Who was responsible for these gliding, effortless notes? He was sure he knew.

Hamish liked his sleep. Normally, wild owls wouldn't have got him out of bed in the middle of the night. But there was something about this singing . . . something compelling . . . *come to me*, it seemed to say . . . *come* . . .

He reached over to his side table and fumbled for the matches in the pitch darkness. By feel alone, he managed to extract one from the box and get it to light. Paw shaking slightly, he applied it to the candle, which sputtered, then caught. Quietly, he slipped from between the covers and pulled his coat on over his pyjamas. Breath freezing in the air, he took up the candle and hurried over the cold floor to the bedroom door.

He pressed his ear against the thick oak and listened. At first, he thought the singing had stopped. But then he heard it again. Sweet, sad and oh, so lonely. It reminded him of young princesses locked up in towers against their will. It spoke of ice palaces, lost lakes and starlit mountains. . .

He took hold of the door knob and was just about to turn it, when a paw landed heavily on his shoulder!

With a wild cry, he spun around, almost dropping the candlestick.

"So," hissed the Professor in a loud stage whisper. "You hear it too?"

He was still wearing his nightcap, but had on a shabby old dressing gown and a pair of down at heel slippers. He held an oil lamp in one paw.

"Yes," gasped Hamish, sagging against the door. "I rather wish you wouldn't do that, Professor."

But the Professor had his eyes closed and his head on one side, listening.

"Is pretty, huh? A little sharp on zat top note, but most promising. I vonder if she knows *Kumbaya*. Vot you say? Shall ve hunt out ze singer? Make musical night of it?"

"Well - yes. All right. But no more

113

coming up behind me in the dark."

Together, they pushed open the door and peered out. The sound of singing swelled. Now, as well as the voice, they could hear the sweeping strings of an accompanying harp.

"Where's it coming from?" whispered Hamish, peering both ways down the long, dark passage "Left or right?"

The Professor listened with his snout in the air. "Right," he said, after a moment. "Down below."

"Funnily enough, I think it's coming from the left. Up above."

"Nein, nein. Guinea pigs haff excellent hearing."

"So have hamsters," said Hamish, firmly. "We're known for it, actually."

They listened again.

"Up left," said Hamish.

"Down right," said the Professor. It was an impasse.

"Let's try both," suggested Hamish. "You try your way and I'll try mine."

"Okay," agreed the Professor. "Ve meet back here in ten minutes. Synchronise vatches."

114

"I haven't got one to synchronise," confessed Hamish.

"Oh vell. No matter. Nizer haff I. Ve count ze seconds in our heads, huh? Six hundred of zem. Zen ve come back and compare notes."

Hamish knew he was right. He prided himself on his acute hearing. Sure enough, as he hastened along the winding passages, the singing got louder. Finally, turning a corner, he saw a steep flight of worn stone steps spiralling upwards into shadow. There was no doubt about it. The singing floated down these.

Funnily enough, he didn't recall noticing this particular flight of steps on the guided tour - but then, there had been so many. After a while, one flight of steps looked very much like another.

Holding his candle high, he began to climb. He tried to keep counting the seconds, but it was difficult. The magical sounds floated in through his ears and filled his head. He had never heard singing like it. His Aunty Enid sang wobbly soprano with the Hamster Choral Society, and could certainly hold a tune - but this was something altogether different.

It got louder as he climbed, around and around, up the never ending stairs.

There was a door at the very top. It stood slightly ajar.

As he reached the last but one step - the singing stopped. He hesitated for a moment, then mounted the last and peeped around the edge of the door frame.

"Hello, Hamish," said Rodentia. "Come in."

She sat on a high backed chair, paws poised gracefully on the harp strings. Candles set in wall niches were the only source of light.

Hamish stared curiously around. Much to his surprise, the room was virtually bare. Apart from the chair on which Rodentia sat, the only other item of furniture consisted of a long, low chest, covered with a white sheet, on which a great many scarlet scatter cushions were arranged. The cushions provided the only touch of colour in the room.

Shyly, aware of his ridiculous pyjama trousers sticking out beneath his coat, he moved into the room.

"I'm so sorry if my singing disturbed you," said Rodentia.

"Oh, but it didn't! I mean, yes, I woke up, but I don't mind. Really. You have a wonderful voice."

"Do you really think so?"

"Oh, I do, I do, I most certainly do," Hamish hastened to reassure her - then shut up, aware that he was babbling.

"Sometimes, when I can't sleep, I like to practice. I had quite forgotten that you were sleeping on the floor below."

"Do you often have trouble getting to sleep?" enquired Hamish curiously. Sleeplessness wasn't something that ever troubled him. Or any other hamster, as far as he knew. Perhaps rats were different.

"Quite often." Rodentia gave a little

sigh. "It gets so cold here at night. Thog always banks up the fire , but it's never alight in the morning."

"Tch, tch," sympathised Hamish, thinking of the cold fireplace in his own room, which hadn't seen so much as a flicker in the last hundred years, if the temperature was anything to go by. "You should get a hot-water bottle," he added helpfully.

"What's that?"

Hamish blinked. Had she really never heard of a hot-water bottle?

"It's made of rubber," he explained. "You put hot water in it. It warms the bed."

To his surprise, Rodentia clapped her paws.

"Oh, how wonderful! You see? I didn't even know such things existed. You know such a lot about the world, Hamish," she added, wistfully.

"Oh, I don't know about that . . ."

"Oh, but you do! You've even been on a train! That must be so thrilling."

"Well - yes, I suppose it does have its moments. The tunnels are quite good. You - er - haven't travelled much, I take it?"

"Who, me? Oh, no. We don't go out much, Uncle and I. I get so bored sometimes."

She turned to him, eyes glowing. "Oh, Hamish, I'm so glad you're here. It's lovely to have someone young to talk to. Come." She sank gacefully onto the cushion covered chest and patted the seat invitingly. "Sit down. I want us to have a long, long chat."

Meanwhile, things hadn't been going too well for the Professor. The further he went down his chosen path, the more distant was the faraway singing. After tramping along a maze of twisting passages and climbing down two flights of steps, he found himself standing on the minstrel gallery, peering down over the rail into the darkness. It rather seemed that Hamish had been right after all.

Feeling rather miffed, he turned to go back up the stairs. It was then that a voice spoke behind him.

"Having trouble sleeping, Professor?"

The tall, thin figure of the Count moved from the shadow of a pillar. The light from the Professor's lamp glinted off his sharp, white teeth.

"Ah! Count! Vot a pleasant surprise. I vos just investigating ze source of ze singing."

"Singing?"

"Jah. As I said to Hamish, a little sharp on ze top notes, but melodious, oh dear me yes, most melodious."

"Really? I confess I don't hear anything."

"No. Vell, nizer do I now. I could haff svorn it voz coming from zis vay, but it seems I am mistaken."

"It was most probably the wind. It whines around the turrets at night."

"Vind? Oh, no, zis vos singing, most

definitely. I vos particularly intrigued, being of a musical bent myself, you know?"

"Is that so?" murmered the Count, coming closer.

"Oh, jah. Music is in my blood," the Professor informed him, beaming. To prove his point, he cleared his throat and hummed the first few bars of *Gerbils In Ze Night.* "You see?"

"In your *blood?*" repeated Ratula, sounding fascinated. His voice seemed to caress the word. "Indeed?"

"Oh, jah! Alvays I am singing. I voz - how you say - bitten by ze bug at an early age. *Polly Volly Doodle, Ze Dormice are Coming, Hoorah, Hoorah, All Ze Nice Girls Loff A Ferret* - I know zem all."

"Well, well," murmured Ratula."This really is most interesting. And would you say your young assistant also has this - er - *musical blood*?" He passed a long, red tongue over his teeth.

"Who, Hamish? Somehow, I doubt it. Tell you vot! Tomorrow night, ve shall find out, eh? Ve haff little sing-song after dinner, vot you say?"

"Ah. Regretfully, tomorrow I am called away on business. I'm afraid that you and young Hamish will once again be left to your own devices. Thog, of course, will see that you have everything you require."

"No matter, no matter! Ve do it anuzzer time. Ve haff a lot off fun. But now, I must avay to my bed. Night night. Mind ze bugs don't bite, ha ha!"

Ratula watched the portly figure waddle away and vanish, with a final jolly wave, around the corner.

He let out a long, shuddering breath. He was tempted. Oh yes. All that talk of blood and biting had brought on the hunger again. But he would wait.The time was not right. The time for feasting was still two long nights away. All Hallow's Eve! The most important night in the calender. The rest of the year one could get by on tomato soup and the odd passing stranger or grizzled woodcutter who was foolish enough to venture out without a pocketful of protective garlic. But on All Hallow's Eve, something special was required. Tradition demanded it. Last year he had been lucky, but this year he had gone to a lot of trouble to ensure that the larder, so to speak, was full. No, he must wait. But, oh, it was hard. So *hard* . . .

Abruptly, he turned and made his way down the steps to the dark hall. Ducking his head, he glided through the low doorway and once more descended to the kitchen, where Thog was sitting at the rough wooden table, peeling potatoes with a wickedly sharp knife.

"So," said Ratula, entering the kitchen. "Have you finished the washing up?"

"Yersh, Mashter."

"Good. Are you ready for the night's chores?"

"Yersh, Mashter."

Ratula pulled out a long sheet of paper from inside his cloak.

"See to the fire. Tidy the wood shed. Clean out the drains. Remove the garlic from the hamster's coat pocket. Rebuild the west wall. I see part of it has come away again. Dust and sweep the vault . . ."

"Mashter?"

"Yes?"

"Garlic, Mashter?"

"Yes. Surely you smell it? The beastly odour is everywhere. I want it removed, do you understand?"

"Yersh, Mashter."

"And, Thog?"

"Yersh, Mashter?"

"Keep an eye on young Gretchen. I don't trust her. I have a feeling that, given half a chance, she may be - indiscreet. I don't want her dropping any hints into the wrong ears. Understand?"

"Yersh. Thog got to watch Gretchen."

"Good. All Hallow's Eve approaches, Thog. All that fresh, young blood within my reach. How can I control myself until then? I am hungry - oh, so hungry. I think I shall walk on the battlements and howl at the moon for a bit." And, abruptly, he turned on his heel and swept away.

"Vot a charming fellow is our host," remarked the Professor, entering Hamish's room with a crash. "Ve haff just had a most interesting discussion about music . . . vot is it, Hamish? Did you find ze source of ze singing?"

"Yes," said Hamish. He sounded doleful. He was sitting on the bed, staring down at his cold feet.

"Vell? Vot happened?"

"It was Rodentia, of course. I had a feeling it would be. She practices at night, sometimes. I went to this turret room, and I sat on this long, low, seat thing, really hard, it was, you'd think she'd get a sofa or something. Anyway, we were getting on just fine, having a nice chat, when suddenly everything changed."

"How you mean?"

"Well, one minute she was asking me to sit next to her like I was a long lost friend or something, then suddenly, she went all . . . I don't know. Faint. Funny. She said she had a headache and asked me to leave. I hope she's all right."

"Girls, girls, who can tell vot girls are sinking?" cried the Professor.

"Yes, but we were getting on so well . . ."

The Professor gave him a kindly pat.

"Sink no more about it, Hamish. Get into bed before you catch a chill. Tomorrow is anuzzer day, eh? Ve haff a lot of fun writing up our notes . . ." he broke off and suddenly sniffed the air. "I don't vant to be rude, but vot iz zat funny smell comink from you, Hamish?"

"Garlic," said Hamish. "It's in my coat pocket. It got a bit squashed when I sat down."

"Vell, I should chuck it avay," advised the Professor. "It doesn't do a lot for you, you know? Especially if you are trying to impress girls."

"You're right," said Hamish, with a huge

yawn. "I will. Tomorrow."

"Now, get to sleep. Gootnight, Hamish."

"Goodnight, Professor . . . Professor?"

"Jah, my boy?"

"Do you think there's something just a little *odd* about Count Ratula?

"Odd, Hamish?"

"Yes. Something about his eyes?"

"His eyes? Vot about his eyes?"

"They're sort of - I don't know. Something."

"His eyes are *sumpsink*? Of course zey are sumpsink. Everysing is sumpsink. Vot can you mean, my boy?"

"Oh - never mind. It doesn't matter. Goodnight."

The Professor tiptoed into his own room, shutting the door behind him. Hamish pinched out the candle stub, which had very nearly burned away, turned over and snuggled down once again into his chilly bed.

I'll never get to sleep, he thought. There's so much to think about.

In two minutes flat, he was snoring. He didn't stir when, some time later, there came a distant howling from the battlements.

Neither did he awaken when, later still, his bedroom door creaked open and a vast, shadowy shape moved quickly across the room towards his bed and fumbled in the pocket of his coat before leaving again, as silently as it had come.

CHAPTER NINE

DIRE WARNINGS AND A DIP IN A DIARY

WHEN HAMISH FINALLY MADE IT DOWN THE following morning, he found Gretchen and Thog clearing away the remains of the Professor's breakfast plates. From the look of the vast pile of dirty crocks, his boss's appetite was as healthy as ever.

"Good morning," said Hamish, rubbing his bleary eyes. "Sorry I'm late."

Gretchen smiled at him. "It's all right Thog," she said, "I can deal with these. You go and sort out the fire."

Thog said nothing. He simply carried on loading bowls and dishes onto a tray.

Hamish sat down at the table with a little sigh. The first thing he had done when he had finally dragged himself out of bed was to make his way back to Rodentia's turret room. Anxious to enquire about her health, he had knocked gently on the door which this morning was firmly shut.

Silence.

"Rodentia?" he had called. "It's Hamish. Are you awake? Are you feeling better this morning?"

More silence. Disappointed, he had tiptoed away.

"What would you like for breakfast?" asked Gretchen. Hamish opened his mouth, ready to let fly with an order ten pages long.

"Breakfast finish," stated Thog.

"Don't be silly, Thog. He has to eat something," protested Gretchen.

"Breakfast *finish*!"

For one wonderful moment, Hamish thought she was going to defy him. and go tripping off to cook a huge fry up with towers of golden toast. But she didn't. She bit her lip, finished loading the tray and began sweeping the crumbs off the table.

"The Professor's working in the library this morning," she announced over her shoulder. "He said to tell you to go up later if you like, but as far as he's concerned you can have the morning off. To catch up on your sleep, he said."

"Oh, really? That's nice. It means I'm free to please myself, then. Have a bit of a *stroll*, perhaps."

Hamish gave her a small, secret thumbs up sign, just to show that he was all set for the secret meeting - but she appeared not to notice.

"Moushe go home now," said Thog, very suddenly. "Thog finish up here."

"Oh, but I'm supposed to help wash up, Thog," said Gretchen mildly, picking up the tray. "You know that."

"Moushe *go*," repeated Thog firmly.

He came up behind her, reached down and took away the tray. She hesitated, gave a little shrug, then hurried off through the door to the kitchen without a backward glance.

"Ah well," said Hamish. "I suppose I'll go and - er - tidy my bedroom. Or something." And, aware of the mole's eyes boring into his back, he retreated up the stairs.

"Psssssssst! Over here!"

Hamish stared around. He stood by the frozen fountain in the middle of the sunken garden. It was Gretchen's voice all right but, for a moment, he wasn't sure where it came from.

Then he saw her. She was peering out from behind an ivy covered statue, beckoning urgently. She was wearing a grey hooded cloak and carried a basket over one paw. He waded through the snow to join her.

"Well, you took your time," she said, pulling him behind the statue.

"Sorry. I had a bit of trouble avoiding Thog, I've got a feeling he's watching me. Look what's all this about? Why all the secrecy? Why do you say I'm in danger? I mean, I know I'm not exactly flavour of the month as far as Thog's concerned, but it's nothing I can't handle . . ."

"It's not to do with Thog. Thog's not the one you should be watching out for."

"Who, then?"

She stared at him for a moment. Then, she took a deep breath and said: "Let me ask you a question. Have you ever heard of . . . *vampires?*"

Hamish thought.

"Aren't they the ones who do the scoring in tennis?" he enquired hesitantly. He wasn't all that familiar with tennis. Football was more his line.

"That's *umpires*. I'm talking about *vampires*." She lowered her voice to a hiss. "Some call them the Undead."

"So - they're alive?" Hamish was confused.

"Not exactly. They're kind of dead, but they won't lie down. Not while they have a supply of fresh blood."

"Blood?" said Hamish., startled. "Did you say . . . blood? That red, runny stuff that squirts out of your knees when you . . . *blood?*"

"Blood."

"Are you quite sure you don't mean tennis balls?"

"Quite sure," said Gretchen, with a touch of impatience. "Look, forget umpires, all right? I'm talking *vampires*. Creatures that roam the countryside searching for victims to satisfy their insatiable appetite."

Hamish stared at her. This was obviously one of those quaint mountain legends that the Professor had mentioned. The ones put about by simple country folk who didn't have the benefit of a proper education. He felt disappointed, somehow. Up until now, Gretchen hadn't seemed the superstitious type. Still. She was a nice little thing. He didn't want to put her down.

"Deary me," he said, politely. "They sound nasty. Er - how do they go about *obtaining* all this blood, then? Exactly? Some sort of system with buckets?"

"Are you being funny?"

"No, no. This is - er - interesting. I'm fascinated. Tell me, do."

"They bite your neck and suck," said Gretchen, shortly.

"Well, well," murmured Hamish. This was sounding sillier and sillier. Blood-sucking ghosts who zoomed around the place

134

looking for necks to bite? Whatever next? Better still, whatever *necks*. That was a joke. He wondered whether to try it out on Gretchen but, looking at her face, decided against it and settled for an embarrassed little cough. "Ahem. Well, well, well."

"You don't believe me, do you?" asked Gretchen, staring at him hard.

"Well - I must say it does seem a bit far fetched . . ."

"You think I'm a stupid little country bumpkin with a headful of daft old wives' tales."

"No, no, I don't."

"Well, then! I'm telling you this for your own good, so shape up and listen, because we haven't got much time."

"I'm listening, I'm listening!"

"Right. Well, contrary to what you might think, Mr Smarty-Pouches, vampires are real, as anyone with any guts could tell you here-abouts. They have terrible powers. They can walk up and down walls. They can even grow wings and fly! And do you know what's worst of all?"

"No. What?"

"Ratula is one!"

There was a long silence. Hamish stared at her. She really believed all this stuff.

"Let me get this straight," he said. " You expect me to believe His Excellency is one of these - vampire creatures?"

"Yes! Think about it! Have you seen him about during the day?"

"Well, no, but–"

"That's because he only comes out at night. Vampires hate daylight. It's fatal for them. They only appear after sunset. Did he give you the guided tour last night?"

"Well, yes, but . . ."

"I bet he didn't show you where he sleeps, did he?"

"Well, no, but . . ."

"And do you know why?"

"Well, if he's anything like me, he probably leaves his socks lying about on the floor . . ."

"I'll tell you why! It's because he sleeps in a coffin down in the vaults!"

Hamish was listening now. Crazy though it all sounded, there was no doubt that Gretchen believed what she was saying.

"Really?" he said.

"Really. I've seen it. Thog has the key. I sneaked down behind him once, and he was polishing the coffin with beeswax! The lid was off, and Ratula was lying in it with his eyes closed."

Hamish considered this.

"Perhaps he's got back trouble," he said, doubtfully. "My Uncle Henry, now, he suffers from that. Always sleeps on a wooden board. Give him a mattress and he'd laugh in your face . . ."

"Forget your Uncle Henry! Look, if you don't believe me, try getting Ratula to stand in front of a mirror.

"A *mirror*? Why?"

"He doesn't have a reflection, that's why." Suddenly, she rummaged in her basket, withdrew a slim, black book and thrust it into his paw. "Here. If this isn't proof, I don't know what is."

He turned it over curiously.

"What's this?"

"It's a diary. It belonged to the last guest who had your room. He was a travelling sales-mouse. He sold feather dusters."

Hamish briefly considered making a witty little remark about them being ticklish things to sell, but saw her face and thought better of it.

"His name was Longtail," she continued, urgently. "His name is inside the front cover, look."

She pointed. Sure enough, there was an inscription written in rather straggly writing. It said:

Private diary of Frederick P Longtail esq.
Read at your peril!

"So what are you doing with his private diary?" asked Hamish, rather primly. He felt strongly about private diaries, ever since his mum had found his and read it from cover to cover.

"I found it, under his pillow. He stayed in the same room as you. Exactly one year ago tomorrow, it was, on the night of All Hallow's Eve. He just called at the inn to ask the way, just like you did. And that's the last we saw of him. The next morning, I went up to the castle to collect the laundry, same as I always do on Fridays. There was nobody around, so I went up to change the sheets. There was no sign of Mr Longtail. He'd disappeared."

"What - left, you mean?"

"No. I mean disappeared. Look, just read it and you'll see."

Hamish gave a little shrug and turned over a page at random:

"*Monday 27th October,*" he read aloud. "*Sold one duster, hooray! Beans on toast for tea.*

Tuesday 28th. Almost sold a duster but pipped at the post by a sponge salesman. Kippers for tea.

Wednesday 29th. Monday's duster returned. Handle came off, as usual. Ah me. Welsh Rarebit for tea.

Thursday 30th. Called into Head Office to pick up new

delivery of stock. Boss says sales are down again. Nothing for it but to go further afield and find new customers. I need to find somewhere that's really dusty. A crumbling old castle, or something. Perhaps I'll head for the mountains. Sausages and chips for tea."

"Skip the food bits," said Gretchen impatiently

"I like the food bits. They remind me of those long ago days when I used to eat."

He caught her eye, gave a little sigh and continued to read:

"Friday 31st. 10pm. I have been travelling all day. I am writing this at the bar of a rather depressing inn in the small mountain village of Grotzenburgen. Nobody is interested in my dusters. though if any place needs dusting, this is it. There is, however, a

local castle. As soon as I have finished my drink, I shall try up there."

"Go on," urged Gretchen.

"11.30 pm. I have been received warmly by the owner, a charming fellow by the name of Count Ratula. He seems very interested in my dusters and has given me a bed for the night."

"Further. Read the last bit."

Hamish gave another sigh and turned to the last page.

"Midnight," he read. "I am getting a bad feeling about this place. The room is icy cold and I can hear strange noises. Right now, I am sitting in my bed, watching the handle of the door. Even as I write, I hear footsteps approaching. Terry overcomes me. The handle is *turning. I can write no more . . . aaaaaaargh!"*

He looked up, puzzled.

"What does he mean, he can write no more *aaaaaaargh*?"

"It's a scream, silly. Isn't it obvious? *Aaaaaaargh.* That's how you'd spell a scream."

"Could be writer's cramp," argued Hamish. "You know, a kind of groan of relief as he flexes his aching paw. *Aaaaaaargh.* Phew, that's enough writing for today. That kind of thing."

"In that case, he would have written *phew*, wouldn't he?" Gretchen pointed out. "*Phew*'s shorter than *aaaaaaargh*."

"Hmm. Yes, I see what you mean. Er - what's this business about Terry overcoming him? Who's Terry?"

"It's terror, not Terry. That's an O and an R," said Gretchen, impatiently.

"Oh. Right."

He stared down at the diary, frowning. The whole thing seemed crazy. He found it hard to get his brain around it.

"And he was never seen again, you say?"

"He was never seen again. Although sometimes, on windy nights, they say you can hear a tapping on the window pane, and a voice crying 'Whooooo'll buy my dussssster-ssss . . ?' And the next day, there may be a feather or two lying on the ground."

Hamish shivered. There was something very horrible in the idea of a vampiric feather duster salesmouse tapping at one's window in the night.

"There's one thing I can't understand," he said. "If what you say is true, why haven't all the locals been - er - vampirised, or whatever you call it.The animals at *The Three Ferrets* - Mr Cropstealer, Fritz, Septica, the weasels? Surely everyone' s fair game? On the menu, so to speak?"

"The Count isn't stupid. There are things he needs from the village. Provisions and so on. Even the Undead need to get their shoes mended and their knives sharpened and their laundry done. It wouldn't be in his interest to turn us all into vampires, would it? Anyway, they're all old, haven't you noticed? It's young blood he's after. That's why you're in danger. He's after *you*, Hamish. And tomorrow is All Hallow's Eve."

Hamish felt the fur rising on the back of his neck. After *him*?

"What about you, then? You're young."

"Ah, but I never come near the castle at night. And even in the daytime, I always make sure I've got plenty of garlic on me."

"*Garlic*?"

"Vampires hate garlic. It's the only defence against them. That and crosses."

"*Crosses*?"

"They don't like the shape. Nobody around here sets foot outside the door without a couple of twigs bound together in a cross shape and a pocketful of garlic cloves."

"So that's why you gave me this . . ." He reached into his pocket. A puzzled expression came over his face. "That's funny. It was there when I went to sleep last night. Now it's gone."

"You see?" Gretchen's tone was grimly

triumphant. "Luckily, I've brought you some more. Enough for you and the Professor. Here." She reached into her basket and brought out a crumpled paper bag. "Keep two cloves in your pockets and put the rest by the doors and windows of your rooms. *Tonight.*"

Hamish took the bag and peered in.

"Tonight?" he said. "But surely, if we're in that much danger, we should leave immediately? Just pack our things and leave on the next train."

"There is no train. There won't be any running until the weekend. The wrong kind of snow, or something. It often happens in these parts. Besides . . ." She broke off.

"What?" said Hamish.

"Well, I was kind of hoping you might help us. It's not much fun, living in the shadow of the castle, you know. Too afraid to go out after dark. Stinking of garlic all the time. Sleeping with the shutters closed, even on hot nights. Dropping hints to strangers, but too scared to come right out and tell the truth in case word gets back to Ratula that someone has been spilling the beans. Can you imagine what it's like?"

Hamish couldn't. Back home, the stoats next door played their music too loud sometimes, but this was Neighbour Trouble with a vengeance!

"It's just that when I saw you," continued Gretchen, "I thought you and the Professor might just be the ones to help us get rid of Ratula once and for all. What with the Professor's brains and your heroic qualities. You just didn't seem like the sort who would hop on the next train and leave us to our fate . . ." She trailed off.

Immediately, Hamish felt guilty. "Did I say that? I didn't say that. I wasn't thinking. Of course I wouldn't do that. Wouldn't dream of it. We'll fight this thing together." He rather liked that phrase. It had a certain ring. "After all," he added, "I haven't got anything to lose. Except my blood!"

"Oh, Hamish! Thank you! I knew I could count on you!"

Her eyes were glowing.

"That's all right," he said gruffly. "I'll go right now and talk it over with the Professor. Between us, we'll think of something. And I

146

must warn Rodentia. She has to know the truth. She must be in terrible danger."

"Ah. About Rodentia . . ."

"She'll be upset, of course, but in the end, after we've saved her, she' ll come to see that–"

Suddenly, he broke off.

"Uh-oh," he said, thrusting the diary and paper bag in his pocket. "We've got company."

Gretchen followed his gaze. Thog was standing in the entrance to the walled garden. His brows were knitted in a fierce scowl. He was holding a vicious looking axe.

"Hello, there, Thog!" called Hamish, giving a cheery little wave. "Looks like we're in for more snow, don't you think?"

"Thog tell moushe go home!"

"I'm just going, Thog," replied Gretchen. Hamish admired her calm. "I was just showing Hamish the walled garden. He's particularly interested in the statues, aren't you Hamish?"

"Oh, yes. I'm a bit of a statue fanatic, actually. Love 'em. Can't leave 'em alone. All those - er - chipped noses and - er - marble plinths. Always been a sucker for plinths, me. Ha, ha!"

"Thog tell moushe go home!"

"Yes, and that's just what I'm doing. 'Bye then, Hamish. See you in the morning."

With a casual little wave, Gretchen moved away. Thog stood aside to let her pass, and watched her suspiciously for a moment before turning back to Hamish, who was inspecting the crumbling statuary in his new role of statue enthusiast.

"Super," Hamish remarked casually, patting the knee of a particularly dilapidated stoat. "They knew how to carve in the old days, eh, Thog? Of course, Seventeeth-century rodent statuary is well known for its - er - famous - er - unique *crumbliness* of design, as demonstrated by this particularly fine example over here which, if I'm not mistaken, is by the well known sculpter Sir Hubert Nostril. Note the graceful lines of the outstretched paw, do you see? And the - er - distinctive absence of the head. Vintage Nostril, I'm almost sure of it."

Still talking, he slipped past Thog, who was staring at the headless stoat as if mesmerized.

"I believe there's a book about him in the library!" he shouted over his shoulder. "I'll just go and look him up!"

Heart thumping, he gave another jaunty little wave, rounded the corner and hurried towards the castle at a brisk gallop.

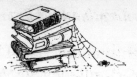

CHAPTER TEN

LUNCH AND A LIST

THE PROFESSOR WAS SITTING IN THE LIBRARY AT a small desk cluttered with tall piles of reference books. Dull light filtered in through the window behind him. In the distance, dark pine trees brooded under a lowering sky.

The depressing view was having no effect on the Professor. He was doing what he loved. His tongue stuck out and his eyes blazed with enthusiasm behind his thick spectacles as he scribbled away, busily making corrections to a floor plan of the castle. He looked up as the panelled door burst open.

"Professor! I've got something terribly important to tell you! It's a matter of life or death. Actually, it could even be in between."

"Ah. Hamish. Zere you are, my boy.

Come, look at zis map. I haff a feeling ve get ze measurements wrong somevere . . ."

"Never mind about that! I've been talking to Gretchen, and she told me something something horrible! So horrible I can hardly believe it!"

The Professor clapped a paw to his muzzle and gave a little gasp. "Don't tell me! Zere is no more fried chickveed!" His shoulders heaved at his little joke.

"No, no. Much worse. Sit down. This is going to come as a bit of a shock."

"I am sitting down, Hamish," pointed out the Professor, mildly.

"Right. Well, here goes, then . . . *Count Ratula is a vampire!*"

There was a little pause while the Professor took this on board. He clasped his paws across his middle and studied Hamish's anxious face.

"Uh-huh," he said, after a bit. "You are, I take it, referring to ze legend of ze ghost or revived corpse who leaves ze grave at night to suck ze blood from ze living?"

"Exactly! Except that it's not a legend. It's true. *And Ratula is one!*"

The Professor pursed his lips and gave a little frown.

"Hamish," he said. "Hamish, my boy. You haff been reading ze scarey comic books, huh? Ze vuns your dear muzzer take avay from you in case you get nightmares, jah?"

"No, no! I haven't!"

"Zen vhere do you get zis crazy idea? Unless you are making joke viz me?"

"No joke. It's true. I have proof."

The Professor looked grave.

"It had better be goot. Zis is serious accusation you are making."

"I know. I didn't believe it at first. But, listen . . ."

And he poured it all out, while the Professor sat with an expression of disbelief on his face. After a while, the expression changed to one of surprise - and finally, deep interest. When Hamish produced the diary, he read it through twice, with a thoughtful little frown. Throughout the whole account, he didn't say a word.

". . . so you see, together, we've got to fight this thing," Hamish finished, wringing his paws and hopping from foot to foot. "Everyone's relying on us. We've got to save them from a fate worse than death. And we've got to warn Rodentia. Somehow, we've got to explain to her that her uncle isn't all he seems. That won't be easy."

He anxiously inspected the Professor's face.

"Hmmm," said the Professor, deep in thought.

"I was hoping you might know what to do," said Hamish.

"Ha," remarked the Professor, clicking his pencil against his teeth.

"Being brainy," added Hamish.

"Vait!" instructed the Professor, suddenly shooting to his feet. and scuttling off between the tall bookshelves. He came to a halt at the far end, polished his spectacles and peered at a shelf which bore the yellowing label *Myths and Legends.*

"What are you doing?" enquired Hamish, coming up behind and staring over his shoulder.

"I am looking it up, of course."

"So you believe me? You think that the Count is a vampire too?"

"It seems zat all ze evidence points zat vay. But I must say I'm very disappointed. He seems such a charming fellow. Ve haff so many interests in common. Castles. Music. Books. Ah, vell." He gave a little sigh. "It just goes to show vot goot manners and nicely tailored evening dress can do. Now zen. Vot haff ve here? Aha!" He pulled a thick volume from the shelf and blew away the dust.

"What is it?" asked Hamish, sneezing violently.

"*Ze Monster Book Of Monsters.* Zis is ze lead-ing book on ze subject. Packed viz informa-tion on monsters of every kind. Let us see." He began turning the pages. "Dragons . . . Elves . . . Gorgons . . . Ogres . . . Phantoms . . . Spirits . . . Trolls . . . goot gracious!"

"What?"

"Zis is most strange. Zere is nussing here on Vampires. Look! Ze page has been torn out! It go straight from Trolls to Vitches."

"You see?" squeaked Hamish tri-umphantly. The sound echoed around the library. Anxiously, he looked over his shoulder and lowered his voice. After all, the walls had ears . . . and eyes. "You see?" he hissed. "That proves it! He doesn't want us swotting up on vampires because *he is one*! The less information we have, the more we're at his mercy! Oh, Professor! What are we going to do?"

"Ve sink," the Professor informed him, calmly, leading the way back to the desk. "Ve put our brains togezzer and ve make list. Ve set down all ze facts. Facts, facts, how I loff facts. Ven ve haff all ze facts, zen ve decide our plan of action. Now zen. Sit down,

Hamish, and tell me again vot young Gretchen told you about zese vampire creatures. I vill write it down."

Hamish flopped into a chair and tried to compose his thoughts.

"Right," he said. "Well, vampires don't like daylight. Come to think of it, we've never seen the Count during daylight hours, have we?"

"True," said the Professor, writing it down.

"And they don't like garlic. Or crosses. And they can fly and walk up and down walls and they sleep in coffins and come out at night to hunt for victims and they don't have any reflection in a mirror and . . ." His voice rose to a hysterical squeak. "Oh, Professor, suppose he comes looking for us tonight? There's not even a lock on my door . . ."

"Is zat all?"

"I think so."

"Goot. You haff done vell. Now it is my turn. Zere is sumpzing zat I remember from many years ago, ven I voz small guinea piglet back in ze old country. I haff old nurse who sings to me before I go to sleep, you know?

Dear old Nanny Sloggit. Vot a treasure she vos. It is from her I get my loff of ze music, you know? So many beautiful nursery rhymes. But zere vos vun I alvays loffed. Now, how did it go again?"

He closed his eyes and hummed to himself. Hamish studied him in amazement.

"What have nursery rhymes got to do with . . ." he began, but the Professor waved him quiet with a flip of the paw.

"Ssssh. I am sinking. Hum, hum, hum. . . hummmm. . . rumpy, tumpty, hummm. . . Vait. It is coming to me. Yes, I haff it! I knew it voz zere, buried deep in my titanic brain somevhere." And so saying, he burst into song:

"*Big bad vampire at ze door,*
Vot a noise he make,
Offer him some hot cross buns
And stick him viz a . . ."

He broke off.

"Now, vot voz it again? Zat last, all important vord?"

Hamish stared at him in horror. What kind of a nursery rhyme was that to sing to a small piglet? He was very glad he hadn't had the Professor's nanny.

"Come along, Hamish, help me out here. Is vell known rhyme. Surely you remember?"

"I don't, actually. All the nursery rhymes I know are full of 'fal de riddle di do's' and 'higgledy piggledy hens' and stuff. I don't think I've heard that one."

"No? Oh, vell. I suppose dear old Nanny Sloggit voz ahead of her time in many vays. Now, zat last vord. Vot voz it?"

"Cake?" suggested Hamish helpfully. "Cake rhymes."

"No. Zat is not it. Funnily enough, I sink it haff sumpsink do viz meat."

"*Meat?* What kind of meat?"

"I'm trying to remember. Don't rush me."

"Did they give him the chop, perhaps?" suggested Hamish, trying to be helpful.

"Nein."

"Did they make minced meat of him?"

"Nein. Good try, but zat vasn't it."

"Well, unless they slapped him around the face with a rasher of bacon until he begged for mercy, I don't . . ."

"*Steak!*" The Professor thumped the

desk in sudden triumph. " Zat voz it! *Big, bad Vampire at ze door, vot a noise he make! Offer him some hot cross buns and stick him viz a steak!*"

There was a little pause while Hamish digested this.

"How?" he asked, at length. "I mean, steak's kind of floppy, isn't it? Not an ideal weapon. How do we . . ."

"Details, details! First sings first, Hamish. You must go down to ze village and buy nice piece of sirloin from ze butcher. Zen, you must go to ze baker and purchase a bagful of ze hot cross buns."

"That's another thing I don't quite understand. Why would you offer hot cross buns to a Vampire?"

"Isn't it obvious? Because of ze *crosses!* "

"Oh. Right. Yes, of course."

"And vhile you are about it, get some more garlic."

"I've already got some. Gretchen gave me a bagful."

"Get some more, just to be on ze safe side. And vun more sing - zis is very important."

"Yes?"

"A bag of peppermints. Strong vuns."

"Peppermints? What, do vampires dislike the smell, or something?"

"I haven't a clue. Zey are for me. I loff zem. Off you go, zen. Qvick, before it start to get dark."

"Oh. Right. Peppermints. Okay. You're - er - not coming with me, I take it?"

"How I vould loff to," said the Professor, sadly shaking his head. "But I fear I haff a slight cold coming on. But do say hello to our friends at ze inn. Tell zem to be of goot cheer. Ze situation is in hand. And tell zem ve vill all get togezzer for musical evening ven zis nightmare is over, huh? You haff ze money? Here is ze shopping list."

"Right. Off I go then," said Hamish, pocketing it dispiritedly. The thought of a long tramp down the mountain through the dark forest on his own didn't fill him with glee.

As he turned to face the library door, it opened with a crash. Thog stood in the doorway with a tray in his paws. "Thog bring lunch," he rumbled. "Shandwich."

"Thanks, Thog," said Hamish, attempting to squeeze past. It was impossible. The mole's huge frame filled the doorway. "I'll have mine later. I'm just popping down to the village for a couple of things . . ."

"Hamshter not go!" stated Thog.

"I beg your pardon?"

"Hamshter not leave cashle."

"Why ever not?" Hamish drew himself to his full height, which brought his head level with Thog's belt. "We're not prisoners, we're guests. Isn't that right, Professor? And we have a right to come and go whenever and wherever we please. Excuse me. I'd like to get past."

The huge mole studied him sadly. He then raised a huge paw and pointed to the window. *"Blishard come."*

Hamish looked at the window. Snow, mixed with hail, was hurling itself at the leaded panes, pouring down so fast from the sky that the view was completely obliterated. It was clear that a trip through the forest was going to be well nigh impossible.

"Oh," said Hamish, sheepishly. "Yes. I see what you mean."

Thog shuffled across to the desk and set down the tray.

"Dish one ish for Professhor," he announced, placing a plate on the desk. "And *dish* one ish for Hamshter."

As he picked up the second plate, he appeared to lose his balance. The sandwich slid off and dropped onto the floor.

"Oopsh a daishy," said Thog, carefully treading on it. "Shilly me." He lifted his boot and inspected the sole. "It got a bit shquashed."

Hamish said nothing. He just felt very, very tired.

"Tch, tch," tutted the Professor. " Zat vos most unfortunate. Perhaps you vill fetch annuzzer?"

"No time. Thog got jobsh to do. Put dinner in Hall later," he growled. "Pig and Hamshter help demshelf. Thog only got one pair pawsh. Mashter gone out. My Lady shick in bed."

And with a venomous glance at Hamish,

he shambled back to the door and went out, slamming it behind him in a meaningful kind of way.

"Now what?" wailed Hamish, wringing his paws in despair. "I'll never get to the village today with this snow! We can't get any of the things we need and we've got a whole night to get through! And I'm starving!"

"It's a pity about ze peppermints," agreed the Professor, lifting the lid of his sandwich. "Ooooh! Cucumber! My favourite! Vould you like half?"

"Actually, yes, I wouldn't mind. But how can you be so calm? Anything could happen tonight, anything! We'll be lying defenceless in our beds, without so much as a sausage for protection, let alone a steak, and . . ."

"Hamish, Hamish! Calm down, my boy. Look on ze bright side. Ve haff some garlic, do we not?"

"Well, yes, but not that much. . ."

"A little garlic goes a long vay. And tomorrow, ve vill sneak ze shopping list to young Gretchen. She vill get ze sings ve need. Now, come. Eat your bit of sandvich. And zen ve vill haff anuzzer look at zis map."

"All right. Where is it?"

A guilty look came over the Professor's face.

"Oh, dear. Forgive me, Hamish, I vosn' t sinking."

"Never mind," said Hamish.

Glumly, he wandered over to the window and looked out at the swirling snow. Things weren't looking good.

CHAPTER ELEVEN

NOISES IN THE NIGHT

"HAVE YOU GOT IT?"

"Yes, I haff it!"

"Are you sure you have it?"

"Yes, yes, I haff it, I tell you . . . vait a minute, perhaps I don't haff it . . ."

"Hurry up, I can't hold it . . ."

"Right, now I haff it . . ."

"I'm losing it, I'm losing it! Putitdownputitdownputitdown. . ."

The huge chest of drawers dropped with a crash, narrowly missing Hamish's toe. They both stood gasping and streaming with sweat, staring at the massive piece of furniture which now stood firmly before Hamish's bedroom door.

"Zere," said the Professor, with satisfaction. "Zat should stop any unvelcome visitors."

165

"I hope so," said Hamish with a little gulp.

The blizzard had brought darkness early. They had spent the afternoon working in the library. Copying out maps and tracing gargoyles was dull work after all the excitement of the morning, but at least it kept Hamish from worrying about the night ahead. Finally, the failing light and freezing cold had driven them down to the Great Hall, where a low fire burned in the hearth and a cold dinner for two was laid out on the table.

It was lonely, sitting at opposite ends of the table, shouting the occasional remark to each other above the noise of the wind, which raged around the castle walls. The Professor, however, tucked into supper with his usual gusto. Did nothing worry him? Not even vampires? wondered Hamish.

He looked down at his own plate. The meal consisted of some sort of pie. It looked all right. Except that there were little black speckles on the pastry crust. What was it? Pepper, perhaps? Or something worse? Hamish thought about Thog down in the kitchen, shoulders shaking with silent

166

laughter as he cut Hamish's wedge of pie, coal scuttle at the ready.

Ravenous though he was, he daren't risk it. With a sigh, he pushed his plate to one side.

The meal over, (or, in Hamish's case, not even started), they helped themselves to logs and kindling from the basket which stood to one side of the hearth. They then retired to their adjoining rooms and began their preparations for the long night ahead.

The Professor's room was much nicer than his own, Hamish noted with a pang of envy. There was a big armchair by the fire-place and a proper wardrobe instead of a row of pegs. The four poster bed looked more comfortable too, with a pretty rose design on the curtains. A tall grandfather clock stood in one corner and THE TRUNK sat in another, its lid thrown back to reveal the books within. There was a four-pronged candlestick alight on the mantelpiece. Best of all, the door leading to the corridor had a proper lock which worked.

Hamish busied himself laying a fire in the Professor's hearth, while the Professor crushed several heads of garlic into a pulp and smeared it carefully around the window frames of both rooms. He then drew the heavy curtains and turned his attention to the doors, which he also annointed with crushed garlic. Soon, the rooms were heavy with the pungent odour.

"Zere. Is done." The Professor stepped back and admired his handiwork, wiping his sticky paws on his coat. "Tonight, ve stay in zis room. Better ve stay togezzer, eh?"

"I was hoping you'd say that," confessed Hamish, with a sigh of relief. He lit a match and sat back, watching with satisfaction as the flame caught. He didn't fancy retiring into his own cold, dark, cheerless room tonight, even with a chest of drawers parked across the door.

"Ve take turns to keep vatch, jah? I suggest ve keep our clothes on, in case of. . ."

"Good idea," Hamish chipped in hurriedly. He certainly didn't intend to change into his fire-engine pyjamas tonight. You felt vulnerable in fire-engine pyjamas. If

- perish the thought! - if it should come to a confrontation, he wanted to keep as many layers as possible between him and the Count.

"Here." The Professor handed him a head of garlic. "Pop zat in your pocket. I save two, vun for you and vun for me. You take ze first vatch, jah? Myself, I am ready for little shut-eye. Vake me at midnight. Sooner, if you see or hear anysing strange."

"Don't worry," said Hamish, with feeling. "I will."

With a huge yawn, the Professor plumped down on the bed. Clouds of dust filled the air as he drew the curtains shut. The springs protested as he settled down.

Hamish flopped into the chair and stared into the fire. It was quite cosy, with the curtains drawn against the wild night and the comforting flames warming his toes.

"Professor?"

"Jah, my boy?" came the drowsy reply.

"You don't think Thog is - you know. One of Them. Do you?"

"No, Hamish. Ve see him in ze day light, remember?"

"Oh, yes. Good. I wouldn't like to be bitten by him. I bet he'd make sure it hurt. I don't think he likes me much."

"Is because he sink you pinch his girl friend."

"What nonsense," said Hamish, with a little blush. "As if Rodentia would be interested in me. Even if I was interested in her. Which I'm not. Although, of course, she *is* very pretty. I particularly like the way her tail curls at the end, don't you? And have you ever seen such long whiskers? And those eye-lashes. . ."

170

A little snore came from behind the curtains. It was obvious that the Professor was either asleep, or pretending.

Hamish didn't mind. He was happy with his own thoughts. He snuggled down.

Yes, it really was quite cosy, watching the glowing coals, thinking about the way Rodentia's tail curled at the end. If he thought about it hard enough, he could almost forget to be scared. Whatever happened, he mustn't go to sleep. That would never do . . .

He was woken by the clock striking midnight. He came to with a guilty start, wildly looking around him.

The fire had gone out.

So had the candles.

It was dark. It was bitterly cold.

And there was a noise coming from the door. A small, squeaking, grinding noise.

Heart in his mouth, Hamish fumbled for a match and applied it to the candle which sat on the side table next to his chair. It only shed a dim light - but it was enough to confirm what he already suspected.

The knob of the bedroom door was slowly turning!

For a moment, he couldn't move. His eyes were glued to the knob, which was moving one way, then the other.

"Professor," he croaked. Strident snores issued from behind the curtain. Slowly, his eyes still on the revolving knob, stood up and tiptoed across the creaking floorboards towards the bed. He reached through the curtains and fumbled about until his paw touched the slumbering lump.

"*Professor*!"

There came a groan, a flurry of movement, then the Professor's face, looking bleary eyed and slightly irritable, poked through.

"Yes? Vot is it, Hamish?"

"The knob!"

"Vot of it?"

"It's t-turning!"

He pointed a trembling paw. The Professor disappeared inside the curtain, rummaged around a moment, then reappeared with his glasses perched on his nose.

"Vere? I don't see it."

They both stared across the room at the door knob. It was motionless.

"It was, I tell you! I saw it."

"A trick of ze light, zat is all. Vy you vake me for zis?"

"You told me to. You said I had to wake you if anything odd happened. Anyway, it's midnight. It's your turn to watch."

Tutting and yawning, the Professor pushed back the curtain and swung his legs to the floor.

"I see you let ze fire go out," he complained. "And ze candles . . ."

"Sssssssh!" Hamish grabbed him by the arm.

"Now vot?"

"I can hear something!"

"Vot can you hear?"

"That," said Hamish, in a very small voice. He pointed with a trembling paw towards the heavy curtain that hung before the window. From somewhere behind, there came a muffled, tapping noise.

Tap, tap, tap! Tap, tap tap!

"Ze vind."

"There is no wind. I think the blizzard must have passed over."

"Moths, zen."

The sinister tapping was becoming more insistant.

Tap, tap, tap! Tap, tap, tap! TAP!

The fur was rising on Hamish's neck.

"Big moths," he remarked, with a shudder.

"Hmm." The Professor sat with his head on one side, listening intently. Then, suddenly, to Hamish's horror, he shot off the bed and strode towards the window.

"Professor!" shrieked Hamish. "Don't!"

But he was too late. The Professor had reached the window, seized hold of the curtain and dragged it to one side.

Outside, a full moon sailëd in a clear sky. There was nothing to be seen apart from vast wastes of clean snow, stretching away into the distance.

"You see? Zere is nussing, Hamish. Just a tendril of ivy, brushing against ze pane. You are right. Ze storm has passed. My! See ze moon. Vot a beautiful night."

And before Hamish could do anything about it, he loosed the catch and threw back the window.

There was a sharp, surprised howl. It came from the side, where the opened window met the wall. Or would have met the wall, *if there hadn't been something in its way!*

The pained cry was followed by a long, slow, slithering, descending sound, which in turn, was finally followed by a soft plop, many feet below.

Heart in his mouth, Hamish sidled up behind the Professor and looked over the sill.

Far below, the snow heaved - and a dark shape emerged.

It was the Count!

"My, my!" muttered the Professor. "So it is true, zen. Ve see ze evidence viz our own eyes. Never again vill I doubt you, my boy."

As he spoke, the Count hauled himself upright and stood, swaying slightly in the moonlight. Then, slowly, he raised his head, opened his mouth and let out a terrible screech of frustrated rage before turning his back and staggering off into the shadows.

"Deary me," said the Professor. "Vot a temper."

"You knew he was there, didn't you?" breathed Hamish, full of admiration.

"Hmmm?"

"That's why you opened the window. Gosh, Professor. That was quick thinking."

"Actually, I hadn't a clue," said the Professor, with a little shrug. " Ze room stinks of garlic, don't you notice? I just vanted some fresh air. But it voz all to ze goot. I don't sink ve vill be disturbed agan tonight. Shut ze vindow, zere's a goot chap. Zere is sumpzing I haff to do."

"What?"

"Sleep," said the Professor, with a huge yawn. And he climbed into his bed and proceeded to do just that.

CHAPTER TWELVE

A VISIT TO THE VAULTS

"ZE STANDARD OF CATERING IS GOING DOWN, DO you notice?" said the Professor. "I suspect ve are vearing out our velcome. Vot is zis muck?"

It was the following morning. They stood before the table in the Great Hall, on which had been plonked two empty bowls and a saucepan containing an unappetising grey mess.

There was no sign of Gretchen. The fire was unlit. All in all, things were rather depressing.

"It's porridge," said Hamish, picking up a spoon. "I suppose we'd better eat it. We've got to keep our strength up."

"Nonsense. Vot do zey sink ve are? Bears?

177

I vant a proper breakfast. Vere are ze staff? Sog!"

"Professor, I really think . . ."

"Yeeerrrsh?"

The gigantic mole stood in the kitchen doorway.

"Ah. Zere you are. Please be so goot as to tell Gretchen I vill haff my usual. Cereal, toast, fried chickveed, grilled tomatoes . . ."

"Moushe not here."

"Tea, pancakes . . . vot did you say?"

"Moushe got shack. She bad moushe. Talk too much. Not do work."

The Professor and Hamish exchanged glances. This was disastrous. They were relying on Gretchen to purchase the things they needed from the village store.

"In zat case," announced the Professor, "ve vill perhaps stroll down to ze village. Find a little cafe, huh, Hamish? Cup of hot chocolate, maybe a hot buttered muffin. . ."

He was strolling casually towards the door as he spoke. Suddenly, he found his way barred.

"You not go nowhere," stated Thog, in a voice that brooked no argument.

"No? And vy not, may I ask?"

"Road blocked. Deep shnow."

"Tch, tch!" tutted the Professor. "Zis is too bad. Is zis all ve get for breakfast? Zis - splodgy stuff?"

The mole shrugged his huge shoulders.

"Thog got other thingsh to do. Important thingsh."

"More important zan looking after ze guests?" The Professor was on his high horse. "I beg to disagree. Vere is your master? I vish to complain."

A furtive look came over Thog's face.

"Mashter in bed. Not well."

"Oh *dear*!" The Professor and Hamish exchanged meaningful looks. "Vot can ze matter be?"

Thog muttered something under his breath.

"Vot? Speak up."

"Akshident," mumbled Thog shortly. "Mashter trip on de shtairsh. Better shoon."

He turned to retreat back down to the kitchen.

"And what about Rodentia?" called Hamish. Unwise, perhaps, but he couldn't help it. "Is she still unwell?"

Thog paused. His spade-like hands balled themselves into fists. When he spoke, his voice was choked with rage.

"Why hamshter want to know about My Lady? What it got to do with hamshter?"

"Well - nothing. I was just asking . . ."

"Well, don't!" snarled Thog. And without another word, he turned and shuffled down the stairs.

"Vell!" exploded the Professor. "Zis is more zan flesh and blood can bear. Such rudeness from ze hired help! I vill not put up viz zis!"

Bristling with righteous indignation, he strode towards the kichen doorway.

"What are you doing?" asked Hamish anxiously.

"I am going to insist zat he cooks us some breakfast, zat's vot. And if he refuses, I shall cook it meinself. I forbid you to touch zat splodge, Hamish. It vill glue up your tummy."

"Er - do you think that's wise? He seems in an awfully bad mood."

"Vise? Vise? Vot do I care about vise? I am hungry. I vant hot food. Never let it be said zat Vilheim Von Strudel let oversized mole in pink slippers get ze better of him. Stay here, Hamish. It vill be better if you keep out of zis. You make him crosser zan ever."

And so saying, he marched through the doorway.

Hamish debated whether to follow him, then decided against it. The Professor was right. It would be better if he kept out of Thog's way.

He wandered back to the table and eyed the bowls. Actually, he quite liked porridge. His stomach was growling with hunger and he almost gave in - but it seemed disloyal to eat it with the Professor making such a big fuss. With a little sigh, he turned his back on it and trailed across the silent hall over to the window, aware of the dozens of pale, ancestral eyes following his every move.

The heavy curtain was drawn back. He breathed on the frosted glass, rubbed a little peep hole and applied his eye to it. Outside, the snow lay thicker than ever. There was no doubt about it. They were well and truly cut off. Gretchen had been their only hope - and she had been banned from the castle.

He was about to turn away, when something caught his eye. Something was moving out there in the frozen wastes. A black, stooped shape was slowly making its way towards him. Every so often it stopped, bent down and examined the snow.

It was Septica - the old squirrel from the inn! She had a basket over her arm, which was half filled with firewood.

Urgently, he tapped on the window. Septica appeared not to hear. She stooped, scrabbled under the snow, hauled out a twig and placed it in her basket.

Desperately, Hamish fumbled with the stiff window catch. For a moment, it seemed as though it wouldn't budge. Then, just as he was beginning to despair, it slid upwards with a grating noise. He set both paws against the pane and pushed - and the window shot open, sending piled up snow shooting from the sill in a flurry.

"Septica!" he hissed. "Hey! Over here!"

The old squirrel looked up, startled. She stared at him and rubbed her eyes. Then a delighted smile of recognition lit up her wrinkled face.

"Is that that you, lad? Can it be? Oh, but tiz a sight fer my poor old eyes! You, with yer dear little innocent face all scrubbed an fresh like a spring mornin'. . ."

"Yes, yes, never mind all that! Look, we need your help! You've got to get a message to Gretchen!"

"All in good time, lad, all in good time. Let me look at yer. Let me feast me old eyes on yer fer a moment. We was only talkin' about you last night, down at the inn. I got me teeth out, an' I'll be frank with yer, lad, they wasn't lookin' too healthy. 'Mark my words,' I said. 'We'll niver lay eyes on 'im again,' I said. 'Im with 'is glossy fur an' the fresh, young blood coursin' through 'is veins . . ."

She seemed set to carry on in this vein for some time. Hamish rummaged in his pocket and found what he was looking for.

"Please, Septica!" he begged. "Just stop and listen for a moment, will you?"

"Oh, but to think that I'm standin' here talkin' to yer! An' I thought you was a gonner fer sure. 'E's a gonner fer sure, I told 'em. 'Im with is shinin' eyes an' 'is pretty manners . . ."

"*SHUT UP*, will you!"

She broke off and stared at him in surprise.

"Well," she said, sounding rather miffed. "Mebbe not the manners."

"Look, I'm sorry. I don't mean to be rude, but this is a crisis. We're prisoners in the castle, and you're our only hope. Please take this shopping list to Gretchen and tell her we've got to have the things on it without delay. Before tonight, if at all possible. Here!" He thrust the piece of paper into her paw. "Will you do it?"

"Aye, lad. I'll do it. You can trust old Septica. Niver let it be said I wouldn't 'elp a poor young innocent like yerself. You with yer plump little cheeks an' yer perky little whiskers. . ."

"Got to go! Heard something!" hissed Hamish, and hastily shut the window. He couldn't take any more.

Meanwhile, down in the kitchen, the Professor had made an important discovery of his own. On arriving at the foot of the stairs, he had been surprised to find the place empty. For a moment, he was taken aback. He stared around, half expecting the mighty mole to come bursting out from a hidden corner.

He then noticed that the door to the forbidden vaults stood slightly ajar!

He tiptoed across the flagstones and applied an eye to the crack.

Blackness.

He paused with his head on one side, listening.

Silence.

Cautiously, he gave the door a little push. Hinges squealing, it swung open, revealing another flight of worn stone steps, spiralling down into shadows.

All thoughts of breakfast temporarily forgotten, the Professor stepped through the doorway and stealthily began to descend.

The air was cold and musty. Carefully he moved on down, feeling for the edge of each step and keeping a firm grip on the rusting handrail that followed the curve of the damp wall.

The steps seemed to go on forever. Then, just as he was beginning to wonder whether it might be wise to go back and fetch a candle, he heard something. It was a low-pitched humming! It came from just ahead.

He craned his neck, peeped tentatively around the next corner, and gave a sharp intake of breath at the sight that met his eyes.

The steps led down into a large, dripping cavern. Candles burned in alcoves set in the walls. And there, in the very centre of the room, was a stone plinth with a long, polished coffin resting on top! The lid had been removed, and Thog was bending over it with his back to the Professor. He was humming away to himself, busily hacking off strips of elastoplast with a sharp knife. At his feet lay a small, white box with FIRST AID stamped on the lid in bold red letters.

At the sound of the Professor's gasp, he whirled around. The Professor ducked back into the shadows and pressed himself against the wall. Had he been seen? He couldn't be sure. Either way, he didn't feel like hanging

around. With a little gulp, he turned and made his way back up to the kitchen. Panting heavily, he sagged against the wall for a moment, then scuttled across to the steps that led to the Great Hall.

"Ah, there you are!" Hamish greeted him, his eyes shining with excitement. "Guess what? I've just seen Septica. Remember the old toothsayer from the inn? I've given her the shopping list and a message for Gretchen– what's the matter, Professor? You look like you've seen a ghost!"

"Coffin!" exploded the Professor. "In ze vault!"

"Who's coughing in the vault?"

"Nein, nein! Not coughing. Coffin! I haff seen it, Hamish, viz mein own two eyes! Come. Let us go to our rooms and I vill tell you all about it." Urgently, he gripped his elbow and propelled him firmly towards the staircase. "Qvickly, lad. I don't sink I vos spotted, but I can't be sure. Today, ve must stay in our rooms. It vill be safer."

"But what about breakfast? I thought you said you were hungry?"

"All of a sudden, I haff lost my appetite," the Professor informed him grimly. "Let us go."

Hamish followed without another word. The Professor had lost his appetite.

Things *were* getting serious.

CHAPTER THIRTEEN

A TIRESOME TIME OF TOTAL TEDIUM

THINGS ALSO GOT QUITE BORING. BEING COOPED up in a chilly room with the lingering smell of garlic for hour after hour was dreary in the extreme. The Professor drew out the tale of his creepy discovery in the vault as long as it would go, and Hamish ooo'ed and ahh'ed and shivered in all the right places and insisted that he tell it again, which the Professor did, even adding little details of his own invention to spin it out even more. Then Hamish in turn told the tale of his own little adventure, which seemed modest in comparison, although the Professor seemed suitably impressed at his quick thinking.

But no amount of re-tellings could fill in

189

the long hours that stretched before them.

They mulled things over until their brains ached - but nothing could be done without the essential items on the shopping list. And how was Gtretchen to deliver them, now that she was banned from the castle? Neither of them relished the thought of another night like the previous one.

Lunchtime came and went. Hamish found a toffee in the bottom of his rucksack and offered to share it with the Professor. The Professor remarked that it was hardly worth cutting in half. Hamish agreed. So the Professor ate it.

The afternoon dragged on. Hamish sighed and wandered around, pausing every so often to stare out of the window and con-coct impossible escape plans. Every so often, the Professor would read out crossword puzzle clues from an old newpaper he had found in THE TRUNK. A red, runny substance that flows around the body, five letters beginning with B and ending with D. Things like that. It was all rather depressing.

Another thing was worrying Hamish. There had been no sign of Rodentia for two

whole days. Could it be that she had somehow found out the truth about her uncle and
was being held captive somewhere in the
castle? Hamish wanted to go and check, but
the Professor was against the idea.

"Nein, my boy. Best zat ve stay here,
behind locked door. Keep low profile, you
know?"

"But supposing he's keeping her a
prisoner? All on her own in a turret room,
trembling with terror . . ?"

"Nonsense. Sog vill not let any harm
come to her. Ze best vay to help your girlfriend is to vait and hope Gretchen finds a
vay of smuggling in ze steak. Ve go sneaking
about, ve get into vorse trouble. Vot is ze
answer to seven down, I vunder? A long,
pointed tooth. Begins viz F and ends viz G.
My, zese crossvord puzzles are hard!"

"She's not my girlfriend," mumbled
Hamish, blushing. But he saw the sense in
the Professor's argument. Time enough to be
a hero when he was armed with a nice cut of
sirloin and a sturdy bagful of hot cross buns.

With a sigh, he turned again to the
window and noticed, with a sense of deep

dread, that the light was beginning to fail.

The hours ticked away with agonising slowness.

At seven o'clock, Hamish found a piece of string in his bag, and they played Cat's Cradle until the Professor became hopelessly entangled and had to be cut free with a pen knife.

At eight o'clock, they attempted a game of I Spy. The Professor's accent caused quite a bit of confusion. After Hamish had failed miserably to get vindow, vood and vardrobe, they both agreed to give it a rest.

At nine o'clock, the Professor complained of feeling hungry.

Hamish felt bound to point out that if anyone should feel hungry, it was him. A small argument ensued. It was clear that nerves were beginning to get the better of both of them.

And then, just before the clock struck ten, there came the sound of approaching footsteps in the corridor outside, followed by a knock on the door. Startled, they both stared at each other.

"Jah? Who is zis?"enquired the Professor.

"Mashter shay time for dinner," came the sullen tones. "You come."

And the footsteps shuffled away.

"What d' you think?" said Hamish uncertainly. "Should we go down?"

"Certainly," said the Professor, sounding firm. "I shall be interested to see if His Excellency has recovered from his little *accident*. Ve still haff ze garlic in our pockets. Ve should be safe."

"But I thought you said we'd be safer if we stayed in our rooms?"

"So I did, so I did. But I haff changed my mind. All zis skulking around is bad for ze nerves. If zere is to be a confrontation, so be it. Besides, I am starving. Ve cannot fight Vampires on an empty stomach."

So that was that.

The Count was already seated at the long table when they arrived in the Great Hall. To Hamish's relief, Rodentia was there too. As they approached the table, Ratula rose and bowed. Apart from a small sticking plaster on the bridge of his nose, he seemed none the worse for wear.

"Your Excellency!" said the Professor. "How pleased I am to see you are fully recovered. Sog tells me you haff had an unfortunate accident."

"It was nothing," replied the Count, with a charming smile and a wave of the paw. "I foolishly slipped on the stairs, that is all. A mere scratch."

"Tch, tch, tch," tutted the Professor sympathetically. And you, my dear young lady? Are you vell?"

"Perfectly, thank you, Professor," said Rodentia. "A slight cold, that is all. Hallo, Hamish. I'm so sorry I haven' t seen more of you. but Thog insisted I stay in bed. He's a darling, but such an old worry boots."

She smiled sweetly at Hamish as he took his seat, leaned towards him and spoke confidentially.

"Actually, I think he's a little bit jealous!"

"Do you really?" enquired Hamish, blushing despite himself. "I wonder why, ha, ha, ha. Erm."

At that point, the darling old worry boots appeared in the kitchen doorway with the trolley and treated Hamish to a look that could have stripped paint.

"Tonight, my friends, it is the Eve of All Hallows. It happens but once a year, and calls for a special celebratory meal," announced Ratula, tucking a napkin beneath his chin. "The first course is a personal favourite of mine. Tomato soup."

"Excellent! Mein too!" cried the Professor. "And ze main course?"

"Ah." The Count smiled a secret little smile. "That, my dear Professor, will be a surprise. You will have to wait and see. Thog! Serve!"

On cue, Thog raised the lid of of the tureen standing in the centre of the table. Fragrant steam poured forth as he busied himself spooning the red, thick substance into bowls.

"How I love tomato soup," continued the Count. "So thick. So red. So warming." His voice had taken on a purring quality. His eyes were glazing over. "The way it slips down the throat, sliding down the gullet. There is

nothing to beat it. Except, of course. . ."

"Uncle, dearest," interrupted Rodentia. "Haven't you forgotten something?"

"Hmm?" said the Count dreamily.

"The toast."

"Oh, goot!" cried the Professor, looking around hopefully. "Nothing like a bit of toast viz soup, I always say . . ."

He broke off. The Count was standing and raising his wine glass.

"Of course. How foolish of me. A toast, my friends. To our last night together."

196

There was a short pause.

"I am sorry?" said the Professor. "Today is Vednesday, is it not? I understood ve vere to stay until ze weekend."

"Ah," murmured the Count, turning to him with a smile. "I fear that there has been a slight change of plan. . ."

His voice tailed off. From far away, there came a knocking at the front door. He set down his glass with a frown.

"See to it, Thog," he snapped. "Whoever it is, get rid of them."

Obediently, the great mole lumbered from the room. A silence fell as everyone strained their ears. Then there came the sound of distant voices, mostly raised in argument. Footsteps approached and Thog once again appeared in the doorway.

"Mashter," he said urgently. "Mashter, I try to shtop dem, but . . ."

"'Ere us all be, then," said a familiar voice. "The Merry Mountainaires, that's us. All tuned up an' rarin' to go!"

And into the room strode none other than Zeke Cropstealer, wearing a rather natty outfit of leather shorts and a jaunty hat with a feather on the side. Strapped onto his chest was a large  accordian. Behind him filed the customers from *The Three Ferrets*, carrying a variety of musical instruments. Fritz the hedgehog, with his harmonica; the three weasels (all wearing sunglasses and toting a trumpet, a

violin and a tuba) and finally, Septica, looking very gypsy toothsayerish in an embroidered blouse and swirly skirt. She was brandishing a tambourine trimmed with brightly coloured ribbons.

"Ole!" she said, doing a tottery twirl and rattling her tambourine. "Doom," she added, as an afterthought.

"What's this?" choked out the Count as the motly crew trooped past, set down their instruments in the middle of the floor and proceeded to

unpack various bags and cases containing music stands and suchlike. The weasels, Hamish noticed, had attached bells to the bottom of their breeches. "What's going on here?"

"Vot is going on?" squeaked the Professor, shooting to his feet. "A night of music, zat is vot! My friends, my dear, dear friends, how glad ve are to see you!"

For a moment, Hamish thought the Count would explode with fury. His lips drew back in a snarl, exposing his sharp white teeth . . . but then, he took control.

"I see," he said thinly. "I had no idea that a concert was planned."

"Oh, 'tidden what you'd call a *concert* Lord Count, yer honour, sir," explained Zeke Cropstealer, reaching into a case and taking out an armful of dog-eared sheet music. "'Tiz just a bit of fun, loik. Us promised the Prof 'ere a bit of a sing-song afore 'e goes, knowin' 'is interest in the local folk moosic. So us thought us'd toodle on up 'ere an' make an evenin' of it. Took us longer 'n us thought to get 'ere, mind, what with the snow an' all. Still - better late than never, eh?"

"Oh, uncle!" That was Rodentia. She clapped her paws together. "*Do* say yes. It *will* be such fun. We've never had a - what do you call it? Sing-song before. Shall I get my harp?"

"That won't be necessary, my dear," said Ratula dryly. "I think there are already plenty of noise producing implements here without further addition."

"But they can play for us, can't they? You won't make them go away?"

"Of course he von't!" cried the Professor. "Vot kind of uncle vould do such a sing? Come along, Sog, make yourself useful. Set out ze chairs, clear ze table, put another log on ze fire! Come along, come along, zis is a party!"

Thog still stood in the doorway, looking wretched, paws hanging loosely at his sides, unsure what to do. Ratula caught his eye and gave a brief nod. The great mole shuffled forward and began to set the chairs in a row.

"You von't regret zis, Excellency," burbled the Professor happily as the Merry Mountainaires began to tune up. "Remember, ve talked about haffing a sing song before Hamish and I bid our farevells.

And now it is happening! Vot luck, eh?"

"Indeed," said Ratula. He had, Hamish, noticed, recovered his composure again. Serene and smiling, he was quite the perfect host. The only trace of annoyance was a slight twitching at the very end of his tail. "Let us take our seats, then . . . I am sure that this will be most interesting."

It was!

CHAPTER FOURTEEN

MUSIC, MERRIMENT AND MUCH MEAT

"US'LL BEGIN," ANNOUNCED ZEKE CROPSTEALER, "with a little number entitled *Reg the Veg*. 'Tiz a traditional song all about our national dish. Take it away, boys."

"An' girl," chipped in Septica. "It might 'ave escaped your attention, Zekey Cropstealer, but I 'appen to be of the female persuasion. Doom, by the way."

"Right. Take it away, boys, an' Septica. A-one, a-two, a-one, two, three, four!"

The band struck up with a rollicking kind of rhythm and the smallest weasel stepped forward and sang, in a high, reedy voice:

"My name's Reg and I likes me veg,
There's nothin' that can beat 'em.
Cauliflower cheese with a pile o' peas
Sit back and watch me eat 'em.
It makes me really savage
When people leave their cabbage,
So eat those veg or give 'em to Reg,
Who'll happily reheat 'em!"

Right on cue, the other two weasels lowered their instruments and enthusiastically joined in with the chorus.

"Oooooooooooooh . . .
Re-fried veg with a little bit of garlic,
Sizzlin' in the pan,
With re-fried veg and a little bit of garlic,
He's a happy man, oi!"

At this point, the weasels linked arms and performed a kind of clog dance, accompanied by Zeke on accordian, Fritz on harmonica and Septica on tambourine. The dance involved lots of clapping of hands and knees and banging together of backsides. It was all very jolly. You would never have

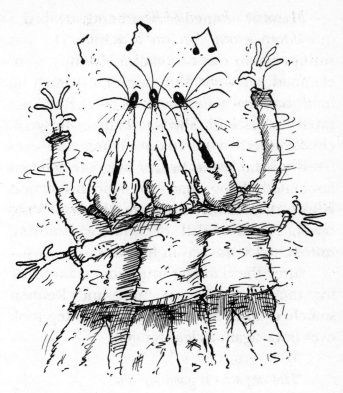

thought that this was the same trio of miserable rodents from three days ago.

The Professor was in his element. He bounced up and down in his chair, clapping horribly out of time to the rhythm.

"Jah!" he shouted encouragingly. "Jah! Zat's it! Jolly, hopping music! You hear zat, Hamish? Zat's vot I like!"

Hamish craned forward and sneaked a quick look along the line at Ratula. He was sitting rigidly in his chair. His lips were clamped in a tight, thin line. If anything, he had gone a whiter shade of pale. Rodentia sat at the far end. She was leaning forward, chin clasped in her dainty hands and eyes fixed on the scene before her. She seemed fascinated. Thog had taken up his station before the kitchen doorway. His jaw hung open. A tray full of bowls containing untouched soup was in his paws.

After the dancing interlude, it was time for the second verse. Luke and Reuben snatched up their instruments and Reg took over once again as lead singer.

"Hot veg stew is good for you
And tasty as can be,
But refried veg have got the edge
And here's my recipe.
Just heat 'em up in butter
And wait fer them to splutter,
Then sprinkle 'em with garlic, boys,
And wash 'em down with tea,
Ooooooooooo . . ."

As the weasels set down their intruments in preparation for another chorus, Hamish felt something light hit him on the shoulder. He looked down, and saw a head of garlic rolling away beneath the table. He turned around and stuffed a paw in his mouth to stifle his involuntary little squeak of surprise.

It was Gretchen! She was peering out from behind a tall suit of armour. She was wearing her cloak and had her basket over her arm. She put a paw to her lips and pointed meaningfully in the direction of the kitchen doorway, where Thog still hovered in a state of shock.

"Get rid of him!" she mouthed urgently, then faded back into the shadows.

Hamish nudged the Professor, who was heartily joining in with the chorus.

"Professor," he hissed out of the side of his mouth.

"*Re-fried veg viz a leetle bit of garleek, Sizzling in ze pan. . .* vot is it, Hamish? I am singing!"

"Don't look , but Gretchen's here! She's behind that suit of armour!"

"Vot suit of armour . . ?" said the Professor eagerly, shuffling around in his chair.

"I said don't look! If you can get Thog away from the doorway, I'll sneak on down behind her and find out the plan. Can you create some sort of diversion?"

They both directed their gaze at the huge mole, who still stood transfixed with the tray in his paws.

"Hmmm. Okay. Leave it to me, Hamish."

So saying, the Professor shot from his seat and skipped purposefully across the floor.

"May I haff ze pleasure?" he enquired, bobbing around under the mole's chin.

Thog blinked uncomprehendingly.

"Uh?"

"Come, Sog. Let us cut a merry caper!"

Firmly, the Professor removed the tray from the massive paws, placed it on a handy side table and grabbed the mole's arm.

"Vun, two, vun, two, come on, kick your legs! Zat's it. Dig zat crazy beat!"

Thog lumbered into action. It was like watching an oak tree dance. Hamish had never seen anything quite like it. The gigantic mole didn't so much dig the beat as shovel it. He swayed and shuffled from side to side, arms hanging loosely and feet crashing heavily on the floor. The Professor tugged at his arm, drawing him purposefully away from the kitchen doorway and into the centre of the room. It was like a very small tug boat towing a barge. The weasels linked paws and skipped around the two of them, trouser bells jingling. At this point, Gretchen made her move. Swiftly, she slipped from behind the suit of armour, ran to the kitchen doorway, beckoned urgently to Hamish, then vanished.

At the same time, Septica laid aside her tambourine and scuttled across to the Count.

"Come on, sir, come on! Shake a leg!"

"No!" protested Ratula, attempting to shake her off. "Really. Kindly desist, madam. I cannot dance . . ."

"Getonwivyer! Yer wouldn't refuse a lady, would yer?"

She tugged insistantly at his paw. Still protesting, the Count was dragged to his feet and hauled off into the circle of whirling dancers.

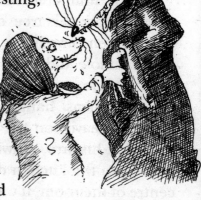

Nobody was watching. Quickly, Hamish slipped from his chair and made a beeline for the kitchen doorway.

Down in the kitchen, Gretchen was hastily unpacking the contents of her basket. She looked up as Hamish came hurtling down the steps.

"Ah, there you are. Listen. We haven't got long. I've got all the things you asked for. Plus a few other things we're going to need."

Hamish ran his eyes over the assembled items. His eyes widened.

"So I see. There seems to be a lot of meat."

"Well, you asked for steak, didn't you? "

"Well, yes. But why the frozen ham?"

"Special offer. Trust me, it'll come in useful."

"Hmm. What's the mallet for? And the nails? And the - er - string of sausages?"

"Ah. That's all part of the plan. Now, listen carefully. This is what we're going to do . . ."

Up in the Great Hall, there was quite a party atmosphere.

The Professor and the weasels had formed a conga line and were snaking jerkily around the long table.

Septica had somehow managed to force the resistant Count up the stairway into the minstrel gallery. Every so often, they could be seen waltzing stiffly in and out of the shadows. Ratula's white face bore an expression of acute agony.

Thog had been unable to get the hang of the conga and was shuffling around in a corner free style, lost in a world of his own.

"One, two, free, kick," he muttered to himself, brow furrowed in concentration, clumping his feet and waving his hulking arms around. "One, two, free . . ."

He froze in mid-clump. He had seen something. In the kitchen doorway stood that hamster! That cocky little hamster who thought he knew everything. He was waving in a cheeky way and sticking his tongue out. And, what was even worse . . . he was wearing . . . he was daring to wear . . .

"*My shlippersh!*" thundered Thog, lumbering across the Hall. "*Get my shlippersh off, you little . . .*"

Instantly, the hamster vanished through the doorway.

"He's coming!" squawked Hamish, bounding down the steps three at a time. Below, the candles had been extinguished and the kitchen was in complete darkness.

"Right," came Gretchen's grim voice. "Don't panic. Here. Take the end of these - and stretch them tight!"

Suddenly he was holding the end of a string of sausages. It wasn't pleasant - particularly in the dark.

He stood at the bottom and to one side of the flight of steps, heart hammering painfully against his ribs. On the other side of the steps, he could just make out the dim shape of Gretchen. The string of sausages was stretched tightly between them, crossing the bottom step at ankle level.

"This is ridiculous!" he whispered. "It won't work . . ."

"Ssssh!"

They didn't have long to wait. There came the sound of approaching feet and Thog thundered down the darkened steps. He was coming so fast that he couldn't have stopped if he'd tried. He gained the bottom step - and his foot came up against the stretched string of sausages. He lost his balance, teetered for a moment, arms flailing wildly - and then pitched forward with a surprised roar.

THUMP! He landed flat out on the flag-stones.

THWACK! There was another sound. It sounded like bone against bone.

There was a short silence. Then there came the sound of a striking match, and Gretchen's small face appeared in the dark-ness, illuminated by the glow of a single candle.

"There," she said, sounding smug.

"That's him out for the count."

She was holding the frozen ham in one paw. Hamish was terribly impressed.

"Wow!" he said. "For a little mouse, you certainly pack a lot of muscle."

Gretchen set down the ham and fumbled at the belt of the felled mole. There came the sound of jingling keys. "Time for compliments later. I've got things to do."

"What things?"

"I'm going down into the vault to seal the coffin. We have to prevent Ratula from going to ground."

"Can I help?"

"No. It's best if you go back up before he notices you're missing. The others are going to keep him occupied until I've finished. The idea is to wear him down. Keep that music coming. Did you see his face when Reg began to sing? I thought he was going to pass out!"

"So - that's the *plan*? We weaken his defences by bombarding him with songs about *garlic*?!" squealed Hamish, incredulous.

"That's it. Then, when he's practically on his knees - bingo! We bring out the steak."

"Wow!" breathed Hamish. "Some plan!" He thought about it. "It's crazy," he added.

"Maybe, but it's the best we could come up with in the time. Go on, Hamish. Go back up and act as though everything is normal."

"Okay. I'll do my best. Are you sure you can cope on your own?"

"Of course. And Hamish?"

"What?"

"Take the slippers off. Go, go, go!"

With a little gulp, off Hamish went.

CHAPTER FIFTEEN

A TEMPER TANTRUM AND THE TERRIBLE TRUTH

IN THE GREAT HALL, THERE WAS A FINAL, wheezing gasp from the accordian and the dance reached its conclusion. Dripping with sweat, Zeke Cropstealer flopped into a convenient chair. Fritz, purple in the face from all that blowing, sagged against the wall and fanned himself with his hat. The weasels collapsed in a panting heap.

The Professor, however, was still full of beans.

"Again!" he shouted. "Vun more chorus! Come on, come on, zis is fun!"

"No! No more!"

The voice rang out, clear and strong.

Ratula came sweeping down the main stairway. He was shaking with barely suppressed anger.

There was a short silence, broken only by the sound of panting as The Merry Mountainaires sucked air into their lungs.

"What's up, yer Excellency?" enquired Zeke Cropstealer innocently .

"It is not my kind of music. It hurts my ears. And I dislike dancing."

"Oh, get along with you!" Septica appeared at his elbow and gave him a nudge. "You' m a lovely dancer, sir. You just needs to relax a bit more, that's all. Try bendin' yer knees a bit."

"Tell yer what." That was Zeke. "Tell yer what us'll do. Us'll play yer a nice, soothin' ballad. Somethin' you can relax to, eh? Come on boys, let's give 'im *Smells.*' Tiz a bootiful tune, sir. You'll love it."

"Of course he vill!" agreed the Professor heartily. He gripped the Count firmly by his elbow and propelled him firmly back to his chair. "Zere. Isn't zat nice? Sit. Relax. Enjoy yourself."

He lowered his voice. "Zey haff come all

zis vay specially to play for you. You don't vant zem to sink you are a party pooper, eh?"

"I said no . . ." began the Count again. But he was outnumbered. The Merry Mountainaires had got their second wind and were already regrouping.

"Our second number this evenin'" announced Zeke, "is a song entitled *My Favourite Smells.*" There followed a long drawn out chord in a minor key, and Septica and the three weasels put their heads together and crooned, in close harmony:

> *"Garlicky ice-cream's my favourite flavour,*
> *Garlic in stew is the smell that I savour,*
> *Garlic on crumpets,*
> *And garlic on toast,*
> *Garlic's the smell that I relish the most . . ."*

The faint strains of *My Favourite Smells* drifted up the stairs. Hamish moved swiftly along a shadowy corridor, on a mission of his own. It appeared that the Professor and The Merry Mountainaires had everything under control so far. That was all to the good, because he was needed elsewhere.

Nobody had paid any attention when he had emerged from the kitchen. Everybody was too busy dancing. Everybody, that is, except Rodentia. Her chair was empty.

Where had she gone? Probably to her room. Perhaps she was feeling unwell again.

He had to find her and warn her. It was time she learned the truth about her uncle, painful though it would be . . .

He reached the flight of stairs that led to her turret and paused, panting. He ran a paw through his dishivelled fur. He must look a sight.

There was a small alcove set to one side of the stairs. It contained a low couch. On the wall behind hung a dusty mirror in a gilt frame. Hamish scrabbled in his pocket and produced a comb. It had been ages since he had spoken to Rodentia on her own. If he had to be the bearer of bad news, at least he could smarten himself up a bit. Vigorously, he applied the comb to his fur.

"Hamish." The silvery voice spoke into his ear. Startled, he whirled around. She was standing right behind him, a pleased smile on her lovely face.

"Rodentia! I was just coming to look for you. I thought you might be feeling poorly, or something."

"Were you? How very sweet of you. But I am quite well. I merely came up to fetch my handkerchief. See?" She produced a tiny scrap of lace and touched it to her temples. "It is getting so warm down there, with all this merriment. I needed to cool off a little."

She sank gracefully onto the couch. Hamish put away his comb and sat next to her.

"Rodentia," he said. "I'm glad we've got a few moments alone, because there's something I have to tell you. Something bad."

"Oh. Really?" Her perfect brow wrinkled and her eyes widened. "What can that be?"

Hamish considered. How was he going to put this? It was sure to come as a terrible shock. There must be a way of softening the blow. Lead up to it gently, perhaps, choosing the right words with care, allowing plenty of time for questions and reassurances . . .

The trouble was, there *was* no time. He took a deep breath.

"Your uncle is a vampire," he blurted out.

There was a long pause.

"I'm sorry?" said Rodentia. "What did you just say?"

"Count Ratula. He's a blood sucking vampire. I know it's shocking, but I'm afraid there's no doubt about it. We've got a plan, though, so you mustn't be frightened."

"But . . ."

"Don't say a word just yet. I want you to look at this." He fished deep in his pocket and withdrew the small black book which had belonged to the unfortunate Frederick Longtail Esq. He held it out.

"It was this diary that first aroused our suspicions. You may remember someone that stayed here a year ago? A Mr Longtail? He was a feather duster salesmouse, disappeared under mysterious circumstances. And we have reason to believe that your uncle . . ."

He broke off. There wasn't any point in carrying on. Rodentia was laughing. Peals of light, tinkling laughter, like bells on a Christmas tree.

"Oh, Hamish!" she gurgled, placing a delicate paw on his arm. "This is the silliest thing I've ever heard! As if dear, *dear* uncle would ever do anything to harm anyone! Is this another of your jokes?"

"No!" protested Hamish, shaking his head vigorously. "No joke. Please, Rodentia, you've got to believe me . . ."

He broke off. He had caught a glimpse of himself in the mirror behind the couch.

Just him.

All alone.

Uh-oh.

Rodentia had no reflection.

His eyes widened in shock, and he turned back to face her. She was still smiling, but she was no longer looking at his face. Instead, her eyes were fixed on his neck. Pale, grey eyes, they were. Why had he never noticed before? Perhaps it was the distraction of the long, sweeping lashes that surrounded them. It was then that he noticed her teeth. They seemed longer than he remembered. Longer - and sharper. As he stared at her, her mouth widened . . .

With the speed of a striking snake, she lunged forward!

And, as she did so, Hamish dodged sideways, brought up his paw and thrust the diary in her mouth! Her teeth crunched down into it, spearing through the cover as though it were made of butter.

Hamish shot to his feet and ran. There was a terrible sound of screaming.

He had turned two corners and was halfway down the third corridor before he realised it was coming from his own mouth.

Oh Oi loves the smell o' roses...

Meanwhile, down in the Great Hall, the final, emotional chorus of *Smells* reached its conclusion. The echoes of the last chord died away, to be replaced by a silence broken by the sound of the Professor snivelling. "My vord," he said, blowing his nose. "Zey don't write songs like zat any more, Your Excellency. Vot do you say? Vos zat not beautiful?"

The Count had been listening to the latest musical offering in stoney silence. He now rose unsteadily to his feet. His face was ashen. Beads of sweat glimmered on his pale brow.

"Beautiful?" he hissed. "You call that beautiful? I have never heard such unadulterated, discordant, inharmonious, cacophonous caterwauling in my life."

The Merry Mountainaires looked uncertainly at each other. They had never heard such an impressive collection of long, unfamiliar words before. But they got the kind of feeling that they weren't all complimentary.

"So you didn't loik it, then?" enquired Zeke Cropstealer.

"Like it? *Like it?* I despised it! I loathed, hated and abhored it. A bunch of cats tied together by their tails has more talent. My advice to you and your so-called musicians, Master Cropstealer, is don't give up your day jobs. Kindly pack your beastly instruments away and get out of my castle."

"Well, doom to you an' all!" snapped Septica. "Come on, boys. Us don't 'ave to stay an' listen ter this."

"I say!" protested the Professor, as The Merry Mountainaires began to pack away their instruments, muttering under their breath as they did so. "Zat vos a little extreme, don't you sink? Zey only try to bring a little merriment into our lives . . ."

Ratula turned on him and pointed an accusing paw.

"No more! Don't say another word! How dare you invite this bunch of hideous noise-makers along to disturb my peace? I hold you responsible for this invasion of my privacy,

Professor Von Strudel. You have made a fool out of me tonight. I shall not forget that. Now, kindly get out of my way. Thog! I need some aspirin! Where is that wretched mole?"

He strode towards the kitchen doorway, with the Professor scuttling at his heels.

CHAPTER SIXTEEN

A FIGHT, A FLIGHT AND THE FINAL SHOWDOWN

DOWN IN THE VAULT, GRETCHEN SAT BACK ON her heels and wiped her brow. It had been hard work, but finally she had done it.

The lid of the empty coffin was now firmly nailed on, using six inch nails at regular intervals. In addition, she had placed a large bunch of garlic slap bang in the middle.

That was it. All the preparations were complete.

And only just in time!

From the kitchen up above, there came the sound of hasty footsteps, followed by a muffled cry and a loud crash. It rather seemed that the Count had come a cropper over Thog. There was a short pause - then a furious squeal of rage.

"*The key! Who has taken the key to the vault?*"

The footsteps started up again.

They were coming closer, descending the twisting flight of stone steps. Any moment now . . .

And then, there he was. Count Ratula, poised at the final bend, staring down at the scene before him with an expression of outrage on his white face.

"You!" he hissed. "What are *you* doing down here!"

"Nailing up your coffin," said Gretchen, with a calmness she didn't feel. "Now you've got nowhere to run and nowhere to hide when the daylight comes. And serve you right, you nasty old blood-sucker, you!"

She thought he would explode with anger.

His eyes blazed and his tail lashed like a whip. Then he got control of himself and slowly advanced down the last few steps.

"And you really think you can defeat me, wretched girl?"

"Not on her own, nein!" rang out the Professor's voice from behind him. "But viz a little help from her friends, she stand a pretty goot chance!"

Ratula snarled and whirled around. He looked from one to the other.

"I see!" he ground out. "It appears there is a conspiracy! Well, let me remind you, my dear Professor, that tonight is All Hallows Eve, when my powers are at their height! It will take more than a couple of anti-Vampire songs and a few nails and a pathetic bunch of garlic to get the better of me!"

"In that case, it's just as well I brought this along then," said Gretchen. And she reached into her basket, pulled out a large, red, glistening piece of meat, and flapped it in his direction.

"Know what this is? *It's a steak!*"

The sight of the dangling piece of meat had a dramatic effect on Ratula. He flinched, drew back and clutched at a nearby piller for support.

"Get back! Take it away!" he croaked.

"Not likely," replied Gretchen, grimly. Slowly, she advanced towards him, holding the steak out before her. "Best sirloin, ten schillings a pound! Only the best for you, Count Ratula! How would you like it? Cooked or uncooked? Shall I fry it up for you with a nice bit of *garlic*, perhaps?"

It was all too much for the Count. He gave a low moan, clutched at his throat and then whirled around, pushing past the Professor and fleeing back up the steps.

"Quick!" shouted Gretchen. "Catch Professor!"

The large piece of raw meat came flying through the air. The Professor held out a paw, caught it and neatly speared it on the end of his walking stick.

"Ten schillings a pound?" he muttered. "Outrageous. Oh, vell. All in a goot cause, I suppose."

Then, holding the stick before him like a spear, he scurried up the steps in the wake of the fleeing vampire.

Ratula raced across the kitchen, hurdling over the prostrate form of Thog, who was still giving an excellent impression of a felled oak at the bottom of the steps. He took the steps, two at a time, emerged into the Great Hall, and stopped in his tracks.

The Merry Mountainaires were arrayed all around the minstrel gallery, leaning over the rail and staring down at him

Each was holding an armful of large, yellow, sticky hot cross buns!

It dawned on him what was about to happen. A little whimper escaped his lips and he raised his paws to cover his head.

"Ready, troups?" came the grim voice of Zeke Cropstealer. "Raise your buns. Take aim - fire!"

"Ahhhhhhhhh!" screamed Ratula, as buns rained down on him. They were hard. They were stale. They had crosses on. They bounced off his shoulders and rolled away across the floor, scattering crumbs. "Swines! Scum! I am allergic to yeast products! Have mercy . . ."

He broke off as a bun caught him slap in the eye.

"Hah!" came Septica's triumphant voice. "Gotcha! Vampires OUT! Vampires OUT!"

Several others took up the chant. Ratula

cast about him, desperately looking for a means of escape. It seemed that every way was blocked. He was trapped, like a - well, like a rat in a corner. The Professor had reached the top of the kitchen steps and was purposefully advancing towards him, stick extended with the attached lump of disgracefully overpriced meat dangling menacingly on the end. Gretchen appeared behind him, raced across the Hall and stationed herself in front of the main door, armed with her frozen ham, which she hefted in a determined manner.

There was nowhere to go but up. Snarling, he drew his cloak about him and raced for the stairs. As he gained the top, two weasels moved forward to cut him off, but he elbowed and kicked his way past them.

There was a heavy suit of armour standing against the wall. With a wild cry, he seized hold of it and sent it toppling to the floor with a metallic crash. The helmet bounced once, then rolled directly into the path of Fritz the hedgehog, who tripped over it, lost his balance and went rolling down the stairs, bowling over the Professor and Gretchen. Zeke Cropstealer and Septica came hurrying from opposite sides of the minstrel gallery, collided headlong with each other, staggered back and joined the pile of armour on the floor.

Cackling wildly, Ratula ducked under a low archway and fled down a long corridor with his cloak flapping wildly in his wake.

Heart thudding painfully against his ribs, Hamish hurtled along a passage. He was beginning to get a stitch. Panic had made him lose all sense of direction. He seemed to have been running for ever. And behind him, ever in hot pursuit, came Rodentia with teeth bared, claws outstretched and a wild gleam in her eyes. If she hadn't been hampered by her long gown, she would have caught him by now for sure.

He flung himself around yet another corner, where yet another long, narrow passageway stretched before before him - and skidded to a halt. For coming towards him, at a vast rate of knots, was a familiar figure.

Upon seeing Hamish, the approaching figure also came to a stop. They stared at each other, breathing heavily.

"Well, well!" hissed the Count. "If it's not young Hamish. Fancy meeting you!"

And slowly, licking his lips, he advanced.

At the very same moment, there came a triumphant screech from behind.

It was Rodentia.

Hamish stood between them, panting, with his back to the wall, head turning wildly from one to the other. He had three options. He could run at Ratula and hope to bowl him over - or he could run at Rodentia and try to bowl *her* over. Or he could run through the small archway in the opposite wall. He had been through that arch before, he was almost sure of it - but where did it lead?

There was no time to worry about it.

He dived through the archway and found himself at the bottom of yet another flight of stone steps. Heart in his mouth, he leapt up them two at a time - and found himself standing on the battlements. Cool air washed over his fevered brow as he stood staring about him, searching desperately for a means of escape.

There was none. The battlements consisted of a flat, rectangular area bordered on all sides by a low, stone parapet. It was the highest part of the castle. There was nothing but a sheer drop to the snow-covered grounds far below.

There came a noise behind him - and slowly, with a sense of dread, he turned.

Smiling horribly, Ratula stepped out onto the battlements.

"Come, Hamish," he purred. "Surely you realise that the time has come to stop running? I have been waiting for this moment for a long time. I've been saving you up, my little friend. And now you're mine - all mine."

There came a hiss from the doorway and Rodentia came slinking forward.

"I think not, uncle. Where are your manners? Ladies first, as the old saying goes."

A Fight, a Flight and the Final Showdown

"Silence, girl! This is *my* moment. I have waited long enough."

"But you said we would share him! You did! You did!" wailed Rodentia, stamping her foot.

Hamish looked at her in horror.

She had changed almost beyond recognition. Gone was the tinkling voice and sweet smile. Who was this shrill, hateful creature? How could he ever have thought her beautiful?

"Don't be ridiculous, Rodentia. You've only got to look at him to see there's not enough blood to go round. Besides, you've been trying to lure him into your clutches ever since he arrived. It was only the garlic he was carrying in his pocket that stopped you."

"So? What about you, then? You tried to get in a sneaky little nibble last night, despite all your talk about waiting for the proper time. It's not fair!"

"That's because I'm the oldest. Anyway, whose castle is it?"

"What's that got to do with anything?"

Hamish, backed up against the far parapet, listened to this in amazement.

The argument was turning into the sort of family dispute he regularly had with his mum. The only difference was that he and his mum usually fell out over things like lunchboxes, whereas these two were squabbling over the small question of his blood!

"Mean! That's what you are. Mean and greedy!"

"Ungrateful girl. I provide you with a lovely home, regular soup, music lessons, a nice coffin to sleep in . . ."

In the distance, there came the sound of raised voices and running feet.

Hamish suddenly felt a wild hope rise within him.

But the two vampires had heard it too. They broke off their quarrelling and looked at each other. Then they turned and looked at Hamish. Ratula moved first. In two long bounds, he was at Hamish's side, and roughly grabbed hold of his arm. Rodentia wasn't far behind. She reached Hamish and seized hold of his other arm.

"Let me go!" he bawled, struggling in their cold grip. "Get off me, you blood-sucking maniacs!"

But it was hopeless. Two mouths opened, exposing rows of jagged teeth.

"Oooer," groaned Hamish, closing his eyes and waiting for the crunch. And then . . .

"*Stop!* Unpaw zat hamster, you fiends!"

It was the Professor. He advanced onto the battlements, waving his stick. Behind him came Gretchen and the Mountainaires, looking horribly out of breath.

"Oh dear," sighed the Count. "Here come the cavalry. Are we *never* to get anything to eat?"

Hamish opened his eyes again. This was a slight improvement. After all, Ratula couldn't talk and bite at the same time.

"You heard!" snapped the Professor. "Let him go zis instant, or it's ze steak for you!"

"What steak?" enquired Ratula.

"Zis steak - oh." The Professor stared glumly at the end of his stick. "Bozzer! It must haff dropped off."

"You see? Admit it, Professor. You are out of buns. You are out of garlic. You are out of steak. And this hamster is out of luck. I've waited long enough. Nothing can stand in my way now. Ha, ha, ha, ha, ha, ha!"

He threw back his head and let out a roar of triumphant laughter.

"Actually, I don't think I am out of luck," said Hamish. "In fact, I think luck just might be on my side."

Everyone looked at Hamish.

"Oh?" enquired the Count. "And why is that, pray?"

"Because," said Hamish - and he paused, partly to play for more time, and partly for dramatic effect, "because you've forgotten one thing."

"Which is?"

Hamish lifted his head and looked to the east.

"Sunrise," he said, simply.

All heads turned in an easterly direction. He was right. The sky above the horizon had taken on a pinkish glow. Far away in the distance, a cock crowed.

Just at that moment, an anguished wailing came from the doorway. Everyone turned to look. Thog stood swaying in the doorway, wringing his paws. "*Mashter!*" he moaned, lurching forward. "My Lady! It not Thog's fault! Dey tricked me! Dey . . ."

THUNK! Gretchen brought the frozen ham down smartly on his head.

"He just doesn't give up, does he?" she remarked as the mole crumpled at the knees and pitched forward for the second time that night.

At exactly the same moment, Hamish made his move. He brought his head around and bit down heavily on Ratula's restraining paw. At the same time, he stamped heavily on Rodentia's foot.

"Aaaah!" screamed Ratula, stuffing his injured paw in his mouth.

"Ouch!" screeched Rodentia, hopping on the spot.

242

And Hamish broke away, running swiftly across the battlements into the arms of his waiting friends.

Ratula and Rodentia started out after him - but as they did so, the first ray of morning sunshine fell upon them. They both stopped in their tracks. Slowly, they turned to face each other, glaring.

"Now see!" spat Rodentia. "This is all your fault. If you didn't talk so much . . ."

"Silence, insolent girrrrrrlllllllll . . ."

Ratula's voice trailed away. Before their very eyes, beginning with the tips of his ears, he began to crumble. He just stood and disintegrated on the spot. It was as though he was made of flour. The same thing was happenening to Rodentia.

As the sun rose in the sky, its rays travelled down their bodies - and wherever it touched, they simply flaked away. The whole, horrible process didn't take long. In a matter of seconds, both Ratula and Rodentia had been reduced to two small piles of dust on the floor.

There was a long silence. Finally, the Professor broke it.

"Zat," he said, "Is ze vorst case of dermatitus I haff seen."

Hamish said nothing. He stared at the little piles of dust. Gretchen came up and put an arm around his shoulder.

"Well done, Hamish," she said. "How do you feel?"

"Not so dusty," said Hamish. "Not so dusty as them, at any rate. Er - have you finished hitting Thog with that ham, Gretchen?"

"I think so. Why?"

"I could really do with a square meal. I don't think I've eaten a thing since we arrived here. How long will it take to cook? "

"Ages. It's still frozen. You'll have to fill up on hot cross buns. We'll have the ham for a celebration feast."

"Er - just one thing? When you *do* cook it?"

"What?"

"No garlic," said Hamish firmly.

EPILOGUE

Picture it. A fire blazes in the hearth of a cosy inn, somewhere in the mountains. Piled platters, brimming mugs, shouts of jolly laughter - all the usual stuff.

There are many things of interest, but for now, we will focus on a large, earthenware pot sitting in the middle of a scrubbed pine table.

A huge, spade-like, hairy paw descends from above and slowly lifts the lid. Steam pours forth in a huge, white cloud, filling the air with the unmistakeable odour of . . .

Honey roast ham. Pink, steaming and scented with cloves.

There are nine waiting to partake of this feast. They sit squeezed together at the table on long benches. They are served by a tenth - the owner of the hairy paw - who reaches between them with steaming plates.

Listen now to the conversation.

"I can't believe you're leaving us, Professor. We're going to miss you terribly. You will come back and visit, won't you?"

"Of course, Gretchen, of course."

"And you'll bring Hamish as well?"

"I most certainly vill. I sink he likes you, you know?"

"Oh, tee hee. Get along with you."

"No, no, really. My, zis ham is *goot*. Don't you sink, Hamish?"

"I don't know. I haven't tasted it yet. It looks like Thog's going to serve me last, as usual."

"Hmm. He seems happy in his vork, at any rate. He appears to haff forgotten his loff for ze Lady Rodentia, do you notice? Just as well, seeing zat zere is hardly enough of her left to fill a matchbox."

Their eyes rest briefly on the mole, who is bustling around wearing his frock coat teamed rather oddly with a pair of bright red, fluffy ear muffs.

Of the pink slippers there is no sign. Evidently, he has transferred his affections.

"Didn't take much, did it?" observes Hamish. "A pair of Gretchen's old ear muffs, that's all. He's devoted to her now. Even though she hit him over the head with a ham. Twice."

"How fickle are ze vays of loff!" cries the Professor.

"Sssh. Master Cropstealer is about to make a speech."

(Banging of spoons and shouts of encouragement. Zeke Cropstealer rises, all smiles.)

"Friends! Us are gathered 'ere today to say farewell fer now to the Professor an young 'Amish. 'Tiz thanks to their amazin' bravery that us can all rest easy in our beds at night, an' fer that, I'd like to thank 'em from the bottom of me 'eart."

(Cries of "'Ere 'ere!" "Hooray!" and "Doom!" from the assembled company. The Professor waves a modest paw. Hamish blushes. Gretchen blows him a kiss. Thog thumps the last plate before him. It splashes his shirt. Fritz takes out his mouth organ and strikes up with a merry tune, which has nothing to do with worms under logs or misty mornings. The Professor wipes the last of the gravy from his own plate and leans toward his assistant.)

"My. Zat looks like a big helping for a little fellow. Do you mind if . . ?"

"Yes. I do."

And Hamish firmly takes up his knife and fork and tucks in.

THE END

BEYOND THE
BEANSTALK

The extraordinary story of what happened
to Jack *after* he escaped from the land of the
giants, the *first* time . . .

"*You know, I've been thinking,*" said Jack's ma.

*Uh-oh, thought Jack. Here we go. Whatever
happens, say nothing.*

*It was a rainy Monday. He was sitting in the
steamy kitchen with the cat on his lap, feet up on
the ironing board, minding his own business,
generally taking it easy. His ma was standing at
the steaming washtub, grimly thumping away with
a stout stick. Lines of wet clothes hung about the
place, dripping into buckets.*

"*I've been wondering which is worse,*" went on
his ma. "*Being poor, then rich, then poor again, or
never having been rich in the first place.*"

Thump, thump, thump! went the stick.

Say nothing, thought Jack.

"I think, on the whole, I'd sooner have just stayed poor. Then at least I wouldn't know what I was missing."

Thump, thump, thump!

Say nothing, thought Jack.

"My beautiful furniture, my jewels, my gowns, my lovely palace, gone, all gone. And it's all your fault - starting with the cow."

Not the cow, thought Jack. Anything but the cow.

"'Make sure you get a decent price for her,' I said. 'Mind you don't get diddled.' Those were my very words. And what do you do? Exchange her for a handful of magic beans! Hah! You should have stayed home and helped your mother, instead of cavorting off up beanstalks. Bringing home all that magic rubbish."

She snatched a steaming kettle from the stove and poured more boiling water into the tub. Clouds of fresh steam billowed angrily around the kitchen

"Wasn't rubbish," Jack mumbled. He couldn't help it. It just fell out of his mouth.

"What did you say? Did you speak?"

"I'm just saying." He had done it now. "I'm

just saying. It wasn't all rubbish, Ma. I didn't see you turning your nose up at all that gold, for a start."

"Don't you be so cheeky! Anyway, gold goes nowhere these days. Palaces take a lot of upkeep. The gold-plated toilet cost an arm and a leg for starters."

Angrily, she started threading a wet vest through the mangle. The way she was turning the handle, Jack had a feeling she wished it was him going through.

"We didn't have to get a palace," he pointed out reasonably. "We could have got a bigger cottage. One with a bit of head height. One where I wouldn't brain myself every time I walk out the door."

"So you'd deny your mother a palace, would you?" cried his ma bitterly, hands on hips.

"No, no! It's just . . . well. A gold plated toilet! I mean! Was it really necessary?"

"Yes! What do you know about interior decoration? What makes me so cross is, we'd still be there now, living in the lap of luxury, if you hadn't let the hen get out. Deny that, if you can!"

Jack opened his mouth, then closed it again. There was no arguing with that. It was true. They had only been living in the palace a matter of months when, one never to be forgotten night, he had carelessly left open the door to the chicken coop. The following morning, it was empty. The precious, golden egg-laying hen had wandered out, over the hills and far away, where the sun shone, the worms were juicy and your eggs were your own to do what you liked with.

What a row that had caused. No more golden eggs. No more wild spending sprees. The bailiffs had moved in, the palace had been sold, and it was next stop: humble cottage. Again.

"I think I'll go to my room for a bit," said Jack, putting down the cat and edging his way through the steam towards the ladder leading up to the loft where he slept. "Work on the Magic Harp, you know?"

"You'll do no such thing!" snapped his ma. "You'll stay here and fold the ironing. I'm bothered if I'm slaving over a hot tub while you sit about fiddling with that stupid harp all day."

"You don't fiddle with a harp," said Jack, in a hopeful attempt at hearty humour. "You fiddle with a violin. Ta-da!"

It was only a little joke. Life was short of a few laughs these days. Of course, it fell flatter than a *cement pancake.*

"Don't you be clever with me! Anyway, all the fiddling in the world's not going to fix that harp. It's broken. You put your great, clumsy foot through it when you came down off the beanstalk."

"Well, there was a giant coming down after me at the time . . ."

"There you go again! Argue, argue, always argue. And mind how you fold that shirt! That's Lord Bellicose's shirt, that is, and he's fussy. Oh, to think that a short while ago all the toffs in the land were begging for an invitation to one of my palace balls and now I'm washing their underwear! From balls to smalls in six months! Ah me!"

And she burst into tears. A big one rolled down to the end of her nose and fell into the washtub with a sad little plop . . .

. . . Jack watched her thumping the sleeves into place and sighed. Poverty didn't suit her, that was for sure. It made her pinched and shrewish. Mind you, she hadn't made too good a job of being rich either. She was probably the only woman in the entire kingdom who found it hard to manage on one solid gold egg a day.

Also available from Hodder Children's Books